AB
F
SHE

The Lost

The town in *The Lost* is based on Glastonbury in Somerset. It is a place of many mystical and historical associations, people looking for other ways of life, self-styled witches and wizards and alternative cultures. Nearby is an area of flat land called the Somerset Levels. It is a fascinating, atmospheric, and sometimes a strangely haunting place.

So the location for *The Lost* is real enough, and so is the incident which begins the book. When I was a child, I was walking to school with my brother and a friend when we saw a fire engine go by. Our friend decided to run after it and find the fire. Of course he couldn't keep up with the fire engine and was soon out of breath. He gave up and we all went on our way to school. But the boy in *The Lost* doesn't give up. He keeps running.

Alex Shearer

THE LOST

ALEX SHEARER

Heinemann

Inspiring generations

Heinemann Educational Publishers
Halley Court, Jordan Hill, Oxford, OX2 8EJ
Part of Harcourt Education

Heinemann is the registered trademark of
Harcourt Education Limited

First published in Great Britain in 2004 by Pan Macmillan
First published in the New Windmills Series in 2006

Activites by Mike Royston

3

British Library Cataloguing in Publication Data is available
from the British Library on request.

ISBN: 0 435 89157 X
ISBN: 978 0 435 891572

Editorial: Hilary Fine, Julia Naughton, Melissa Okusanya
Design: Phil Leafe

Typeset by Thomson, India and TechType, Oxon

Cover design by Forepoint

Printed in China by CTPS

Cover photo: © Getty Images

Deep into the lone wood the stranger went, as behind him the children followed. Then the forest closed around them, and the Piper and the children were gone. Yet there was one that was left behind.

(Old Tale)

Chapter 1

Siren

They were on their way to school when it happened.

They were walking along by the crossing when the fire engine went past and Jonah said, 'Come on! Let's follow it! Let's find the fire!' And he pelted off down the road. Joe Langley ran after him, shouting, 'No, no, we'll be late for school! Come back!'

But Jonah didn't, so Joe had to run after him as Jonah chased after the fire engine and the fire engine disappeared over the hill.

'We'll never catch it!' Joe shouted.

'It might stop at the traffic lights!'

'Fire engines don't stop for traffic lights. The only thing they stop for is fires!'

It was a ludicrous idea and Joe knew it was, even if Jonah didn't. Jonah saw something, he wanted it, and after it he went. The impossibility of achieving his ambitions never entered his head. He always wanted what couldn't be had, yet even when he didn't get it he didn't seem disappointed. He just focused his mind on something else equally unattainable and pursued that instead.

'Let's get the bikes!' Jonah shouted. 'We might be able to keep up with it if we get the bikes.'

But Joe couldn't even keep up with Jonah. He had a stitch in his side already and the effort of running was starting to hurt, the deep breaths of air searing his lungs. Anyway, how *could* they get the bikes? They'd have to go home first and that would take even longer. By the time they'd done that, the fire engine could be anywhere. And what if Joe's mum was home and she saw him back for his bike and not in school like he should be? He'd be up to his neck in trouble then.

'Come on!'

Joe could feel himself slowing.

'Jonah! There's no point! Be realistic.'

But realism wasn't Jonah's strong point.

And besides, as far as trouble went, there was more than one way of getting into it. If they went on running after the fire engine, they'd be late for school and get into trouble that way. That was the thing about trouble – it had a lot of entrances, but not many exits. In fact, trouble was a one-way street.

Joe stopped, out of breath, hot and winded, and filled with a sense of pointlessness. He'd had enough.

'Jonah! Come back! We'll never catch it. Come on. Let's go to school.'

But Jonah ignored him and ran on. He looked back once from the corner of the road, his mouth a wide grin, his eyes full of all the fun, defiance and sheer delight of it.

'Come on, Langy!'

Joe stood where he was, out of breath, panting, worried and afraid of trouble – just like always – cautious and holding back.

'No, Jonah! Come back! Let's go to school!'

'Well, if you're not coming, don't tell 'em where I've gone, all right? Don't tell 'em! Promise?'

Joe nodded reluctantly. Jonah grinned and waved and then turned and ran on, haring off in the direction of the fire engine, which could still be heard if no longer seen. Its screaming siren announced its route and Jonah ran after it like a dog after a rabbit. He was gone from sight, away into the warren of back streets and alleys, up to the Five Ways roundabout and then finally out into the surrounding countryside. He saw the engine again, a streak of red, far away up on the hill.

Going to the country, Jonah thought. Must be a farm, a barn maybe, a hayrick on fire.

He ran on. It would stop soon and he would catch it up. He was quite convinced of that. As he ran he looked to the horizon, searching for some telltale plume of smoke that would give the location of the fire. He could see none. Maybe it was a false alarm, or an exercise to keep the firemen on their toes and stop them getting bored. Maybe it wasn't a fire at all. Maybe it was an accident, a pile-up on the motorway. They sent fire engines to road accidents, he knew that from the news. You saw pictures in the papers. They'd be there spraying foam on to dangerous chemicals that had spilled from tankers, or they'd be getting people out of the wreckage of cars.

Even if it was an accident and not a fire it was still worth seeing. So on he ran. He'd forgotten all about school now, about the trouble he'd get into for being late, about what his gran would say – about him being a handful and too much for an old woman to bring up on her own. He'd forgotten about Joe, about Miss Robertson, about mid-morning break, about lunch, about games, about everything. All he could think of was getting there, and seeing what there was to see, and then he could picture himself telling everyone afterwards – 'I saw the fire!' They'd all be wishing they'd seen it too, but they wouldn't have done, because they didn't have it in them to run after the fire engine as it screamed by with sirens blaring. They'd never have thought of it or, if they had, they'd never have done it. Having ideas was only a part of it; putting them into practice was the real thing.

On he ran. The town was behind him now and farms were ahead. The siren had faded or maybe even been turned off. But it couldn't be that far away, could it?

Anyway, he wasn't going to school now, no matter what. He couldn't. Even if he turned back, he'd never get there in time. It was easier to take the whole day off now than to go in late and make excuses which nobody would ever believe. He'd get a note from Gran for tomorrow or just write one himself. He could say he'd been sick. There was only Joe who knew that he wasn't, and he wouldn't say anything. Joe might even do him a favour and put a tick in the register later when Miss Robertson wasn't looking. She'd never remember. She always had too much on her mind, what with class sizes being as big as they were, as she was always saying.

Jonah seemed to be leaving everything behind him, not just this Tuesday morning and the usual ways of passing it and of doing things – not just the town either. He was leaving more than that. He felt as if he were running to paradise and abandoning everything he had ever known in exchange for a better life. It was as if the fire engine were a Pied Piper, and its siren and lights its song of enchantment. As if it were leading him away from Hamelin to a place where life would be better and happier and full of interest and excitement. It would be a shame not to see Gran any more of course, and Dad on his rare visits, and Joe too and the rest of his friends. But something had to be lost for something else to be gained. Gran was getting old now anyway, and always complaining about her creaking joints and not having enough money and how she shouldn't be bringing up children again, not at her time of life.

She was all right though was Gran, in her way. It was just that her way was an old, slow, boiled-cabbage-and-too-many-cats sort of way. It wasn't what he wanted. He wanted something light and airy and full of freedom.

So Jonah ran on. It was hardly any effort to him. He felt as if he could run and run, even if the fire was a marathon away. He'd find it and, when he found it, there would be

4

something important for him there. Maybe he would save somebody, do something heroic. Maybe he would find something in amongst the smouldering ruins. In his imagination he could see the water pouring from the fire hoses in great arcs; he could hear the sizzle of the water on the embers; he could smell the acrid smoke and hear the cries of frightened animals. Whatever awaited him it was fate, destiny, what he had been born for. So on he ran.

At last he grew tired, despite his earlier feelings of invincibility. He slowed and jogged a while, then stopped completely. He walked a bit, then began to jog again. He had gone a few miles now, but there was still nothing to mark the whereabouts of the fire. No smoke without fire, people said. But could there be a fire without smoke?

Back in the classroom Miss Robertson was calling the register.

'Jonah Byford?'

There was no reply.

'Does anyone know where Jonah is? Is he late? Or ill?' There was silence. 'Has anyone seen him this morning?'

Joe Langley shook his head along with the rest. He didn't want to get his friend into trouble. Maybe if he had said something then, it might have been different later. He wouldn't have had the burden of all the nightmares and the guilt. It wouldn't have felt like it was all his fault.

He should have told the truth – something that would have absolved him. He should have put his hand up and said, 'I think I might have seen him earlier, miss. He was running after a fire engine.'

'He was *what*, Joseph?' she would have said, her face lighting up with incredulity. Every child in the class would have turned and stared – some of them with big smiles on their faces.

So Jonah had run after a fire engine – to find a fire? Only Jonah would ever think he could catch a fire engine. And, knowing him, he probably would too.

Yes, Joe should have told the truth, and Miss Robertson would have done something. She would have gone and had a word with Mr Jeft, the headmaster, and that would have been it. The head would have had to decide what to do then and how seriously to take it and, knowing him and how worried he'd be about getting into hot water if he didn't do anything, he'd probably have rung up Jonah's gran amongst other people, and someone would have gone after Jonah and brought him back.

Then it would all have been different. Probably. Or maybe it would already have been too late.

But Joe didn't say a word. He sat there, mute with conspiracy, not betraying a confidence, staying loyal to his friend.

'Joe Langley – you're good friends with Jonah. Did you see him on your way to school this morning?'

'No, miss. Not today.'

'OK then. He must be ill. I'll check with the office later. Maybe his gran's rung up to say he's poorly and won't be coming in. Right. Rachael Cross?'

'Here, miss!'

She went on through the register, then closed it and put it away.

'OK, let's get on now. If you'd open up your geography books at page…'

And lessons began.

So that was it. That was how it happened. Jonah went and ran after a fire engine.

He was never seen again.

Chapter 2

The Stranger

He must have talked to a stranger. That had to be what had happened. You weren't supposed to talk to strangers, everybody knew that. It was the first thing they warned you about, right from the word go.

But why would Jonah have talked to a stranger when he knew not to, same as everyone did? All right, to start with because he was the kind of person who *would* talk to strangers, and make friends with them too. Come to that, how did you ever make any friends if you didn't talk to strangers? Everybody is a stranger when you first meet them.

Only they didn't mean that of course. There were different kinds of strangers and some were stranger than others. It was the strange kind of strangers you had to worry about – or maybe not. Your parents would tell you it was often the nice ones – who seemed pleasant and sincere – that could be the most dangerous. They only acted like that to win your confidence, and then, before you knew it...

What?

That was all left to your imagination.

But Jonah wasn't stupid. He might have talked to a stranger but he wouldn't have gone anywhere with one. He wouldn't have accepted a lift in a car or have fallen for that one about 'Your mother's in hospital and I'm to take you to see her right now. It's urgent, so if you just get in the back ...' It wouldn't have worked. He didn't have a mum, just his gran, and his dad occasionally. And even if he had, he still wouldn't have gone. He had too much sense. Unless they were bigger than he was, and they would have been, naturally, but even then...

But it was the only possible explanation – that he'd gone with a stranger. He couldn't have just evaporated and vanished off the face of the earth.

Jonah's absence wasn't noticed until around six o'clock. His gran had got tea ready and he hadn't turned up to eat it. School had finished hours ago, but Jonah often went round to Joe's house afterwards. Joe's mum said they were inseparable and as good as twins, or at least blood brothers – why, even their names were alike.

But if Jonah was eating there he'd always ring up to say so, and he hadn't. If he wasn't at Joe's he might have stayed behind at school for some extra-curricular activity or gone to play football in the park. But, in that case, he was usually back by six at the latest. His stomach wouldn't let him stay out longer. It commanded him to go home and eat.

His gran fretted for a while but she wasn't overly given to anxiety. Her own children had grown up in a different world; they'd had plenty of freedom. They'd stayed out late on summer evenings, with not even a mobile phone to ring home on. It was all so different then. The world had been safer, or at least it had been perceived as such. There had always been strangers though, even then, but quite often you laughed about them, like at the funny man who hung around the park shelter and offered you money to do things. Everyone laughed at him and mostly stayed out of his way, or they had a name to tease him with. He'd get angry and run after the boys who called him things, but he was too slow ever to catch them. Even danger hadn't seemed so dangerous back then. Or there had been other, bigger, more pressing dangers to worry about, like the war and bombs.

By the time seven came she started to worry. She went out and knocked on the neighbour's door. The young man, Donald, came out, and he wasn't that pleased to see her just then as he was putting up some shelves in what was going to be the study, but he could see that she was agitated so he asked her in and, while Gina made her a cup of tea and tried to calm her, he started to ring around the various places Jonah might have gone to. Then he rang the police. They came quite quickly, within ten minutes or so. He was listening out for the siren but he didn't hear one. There was just a ring at the doorbell, and then there they were.

They took a statement and began making telephone calls too. One of the first people they rang was Mr Jeft, the headmaster, who said he'd go straight back to the school and check the day's register. In the meantime he gave them the number of Miss Robertson. She wasn't at home but she had left her mobile on and it went off in the cinema, to the irritation of everyone around her and to the embarrassment of the friend she had gone with. She hurried out of the cinema, her face burning, and took the call in the foyer.

That was when they discovered that Jonah had not been at school that day. That he wasn't just an hour or two late. It wasn't just a schoolboy who had forgotten the time. It was far more serious than that. He wasn't just late, he was missing. He hadn't been seen since the morning.

They asked Jonah's gran what he had been wearing and carrying when he had left home. She described it to them; it was the usual school sweatshirt and jeans, the usual backpack, and as far as she knew he had gone straight to school, though he might have met up with Joe Langley on the way, as they often walked in together. They also asked if Jonah carried a mobile phone, but she had never got round to buying him one; she'd managed

9

without one when she was a girl – they'd never had such things – and she didn't believe in them now.

Two police officers turned up at Joe's house to talk to him, shortly before he was due to go to bed. But a petrified Joe claimed that he hadn't seen Jonah that morning, that, yes, they did usually walk in together, but today they had somehow missed each other. He couldn't say Jonah had legged it after the fire engine. He couldn't get him into trouble, could he? He'd promised Jonah not to tell on him, and a promise was a promise. And, anyway, Jonah would surely get home any moment now?

When Joe woke the next morning, he hurried downstairs to ask his mother if there was news of Jonah yet. When she said no, his reaction was fear. He felt his skin turn cold and all he could think of was going on avoiding trouble. He didn't want to get into it, and he wanted to keep Jonah out of it. It was still best not to say anything, he decided that almost immediately. If he kept quiet, nobody would know that Jonah had gone skiving – wherever he now was or whatever he was doing. Then when Jonah came back he could make his own excuses and there would be nothing to contradict him.

Only where could he have gone that he would have stayed out all night? A million places, knowing Jonah – well, a thousand anyway. He was as random as a billiard ball hitting the soft, green-baize cushion. He could have gone off in any direction, then gone and bounced off something else, and there'd be no telling where he might end up.

He might have realised that he could never keep up with the fire engine and have found himself miles outside town. It would have been too late to go back to school without getting into trouble by then, so he might have decided to go exploring, or just to go wandering along the willow banks, or nosing around where the travellers were, with their lorries and caravans and converted ambulances and their peace and love and 'no war in my name' stickers on their rusting cars.

He could have sat there all day and then stayed overnight, camping out in a borrowed sleeping bag. They wouldn't have cared. They'd have thought it was a laugh. They'd have made him tea, boiling up a kettle on a Primus stove. They'd have let him try to play one of the out-of-tune guitars, or ride round on a cobbled-together bicycle, made up from parts recovered from the scrapyard and dragged out of skips. The travellers didn't seem to place much value on things like education – well, not the formal kind anyway. Their children ran mucky and half naked around the site, scratching their heads and playing with the ashes of dead fires, crying when the dust got in their eyes, sneezing and coughing and doing it again.

Where else could Jonah be? On one of the farms maybe. He could have hidden out in a barn, spent the night there. Only he'd have gone hungry doing that and Jonah didn't like to go hungry. But he could have pinched something – a cake cooling on a window ledge … if cakes did still cool on window ledges.

He'd have found something though. Or one of the farmers might have given him something to do – something not too hard and not too dangerous, what with all the rules and regulations. He could have helped with the sheep, numbering the lambs, daubing red or blue marks on them so they didn't get mixed up with the lambs from other farms.

The farmers were a bit like the travellers – though they hated them for the most part. What they had in common was, if not a lack of respect for formal education, at least a cynical view of it. They respected educated people well enough, especially when they were useful ones – vets, doctors, lawyers, people like that. But too many educated people had no common sense, no practical use to them. They didn't even know how to deliver a lamb or hitch up a tractor and trailer. Why did you need to know about the Battle of Hastings or French irregular verbs when the cattle were bloated with too much grass and the only cure was to stick a knife in the side of them to let out all the gas?

Where else could Jonah have gone? The police thought he might have gone to visit his dad, but when they checked they couldn't even get hold of him; he had gone away on some building job and wasn't expected back for days.

The speculation grew darker. An accident, of course, that was always a possibility. Jonah was reckless, a risk taker, the first up to the high branches and the first to jump all the way down. He might have hurt himself, fractured something, landed badly. He might have lain overnight in a ditch or across a tree stump, his leg or ribs broken.

Well, they'd find him then, wouldn't they. If he didn't turn up soon the police would start scouring the countryside with tracker dogs and all the rest. They'd see him or they'd hear him moaning or one of the dogs would discover him. How would it help anyway, for Joe to tell anyone about Jonah running after the fire engine? What good was that going to do, other than to land him in deeper and hotter water the moment he was found? Jonah would never forgive him if Joe landed him in the muck. You had to stay loyal to your friends.

So Joe stuck with his resolution not to say anything, though he knew that as Jonah's best friend the police would want to talk to him again – and sooner rather than later. But he wasn't going to let a mate down. He wasn't one to betray a confidence or drop Jonah in the soup. The others in his class could say whatever they wanted, but Joe was staying loyal – and silent.

He'd give it till the afternoon, or this evening perhaps. If Jonah hadn't turned up by then, he'd tell his mother the truth and she could ring the police. But he wasn't going to get Jonah into any more trouble than he was in already.

So, not fully intending to, Joe let a whole day go by, worried sick, but delaying and waiting every moment for Jonah to come home. The longer he left it, the harder it became to say anything. Now he would have his own lies to explain. Now he would be in trouble as well. It wasn't just Jonah, it was him too. It was better to keep silent, for both their sakes.

When Joe woke the following morning, it was nearly forty-eight hours since Jonah had set off after the fire.

The police had talked to all Jonah's classmates by now, but had received no useful information from anyone, so at first light they began the search. They were joined by various volunteers, some of the travellers and farmers among them. They combed the ditches and thickets and looked in all the outhouses and barns.

The reason the farmers didn't like the travellers was because they weren't above encroaching on the farmers' land, setting up camps where they felt like it. Then it was no easy matter to dislodge them. It took more than threats and raised voices; it took time and legal proceedings. They could be there for months, turning the place into a tip. A lot of them came for the festival, which was held every couple of years. They came and they never left. Drug addicts and layabouts too, half of them, or so the farmers believed, living on benefits and leaving nothing but mess and squalor behind them.

So the farmers disliked the travellers, and the travellers disliked the police; yet here they were now, searching alongside each other for the missing boy.

Jonah's picture was on the morning news when Joe came down for breakfast on Thursday. His mother said that she didn't really like television and only had it for the wildlife programmes, but as far as he could tell it was always on, and anyway, today was different.

'Look, there he is…' she said as Jonah's picture came up on the screen. The police had got it from his grandmother. It had been cropped from a class photograph of a few months ago. The tall people were at the back, the shorter ones at the front. Jonah was at the end of the second row from the back. If they had shown the whole photograph on the television, you could have seen that Joe Langley was standing next to him.

He felt colder than ever, his whole body turned to ice.

The TV announcer was talking over the picture.

'Jonah Byford was last seen on Tuesday morning when he left home to go to school. Anyone who might have seen him or who may have any relevant information…'

That was Joe, and he knew it. He had seen him; he had all the relevant information and he had kept it to himself.

'You all right?' his mother said, looking at him strangely.

'Sure. I'm fine.'

'I wonder what could have happened to him?' Joe's mother said, watching him closely. 'I'm surprised you didn't see him on Tuesday morning. Don't you always walk to school together?'

'Not every day.'

'Are you sure you didn't see him, Joe?'

'I'd have said, wouldn't I? I'd have told them if I had!'

He blushed scarlet. His mother saw he was upset and she said gently, 'You mustn't worry now, Joe, they'll find him. He's probably just run away for a while, you know, the way kids sometimes do.'

Yes, he did know. Only the way people did it – at least people of Jonah's age – was not to run away at all. They usually went as far as the end of the road with a packet of biscuits taken from the kitchen cupboard and maybe a carton of milk. Then they sat on a wall and waited to be missed. They nibbled at a biscuit or two and again felt all the anger, the unfairness and the sense of injustice which had driven them away, feeling that home was a prison and their families their jailers – not knowing that they were being watched with amused concern from the bedroom window back down the street.

That kind of running away was all a game – a game of waiting for somebody to come and show that they loved you and that they wanted you to come home.

Sometimes they went further than the end of the road – maybe even to the park or beyond. But hunger and the night usually drove them back and they would return, a little sheepishly, to find welcome and forgiveness. Then there would be apologies on both sides and some kind of reconciliation, followed by hot drinks and a warm bath and the luxury of a soft, safe bed.

That was what running away usually consisted of. You didn't stay out all night and still be missing the next morning, and the morning after that. That was serious running away, grown-up running away. That was running away with attitude.

Joe's mother thought that in the circumstances – with a full-scale search on now – school might be cancelled, so she rang up to check, but it wasn't. She gave him the option of staying at home though, but he didn't want to, so – uncharacteristically – she said she would walk him in.

They were all being walked in.

Why? Joe wondered. Were they expecting the same thing to happen again immediately? Had the danger been any less last week, or a year ago?

They were all talking about it too, all the mothers and fathers.

'I wonder what could have happened to him?'

'I hope they find him…'

But, of course, everybody hoped that.

'I mean, in a place like this. It's not the city…'

Which was true enough. It was just a small country town – unique and in its way rather eccentric. Its past and its history 'attracted the wrong sort', some people believed, and the wrong sort it attracted were the ones who bought the rune stones and the quartz jewellery and the packs of tarot cards and the crystal balls from the shops on the High Street. Or they frequented the hemp shop, which sold hemp jeans and T-shirts and even hemp underwear, and packets of cannabis seeds. The man behind the counter went on buying trips to Amsterdam.

Practically every other shop sold weird stuff – things to do with mysticism and strange, ancient religions. You could do an evening class in witchcraft (so the board outside the organic cafe and learning centre said); you could get clothes from India and buy little brass pots, bottles of patchouli oil, and sandalwood soap cut in rough, uneven chunks. If you were sick at heart, there was the Soul Therapy Centre, where you could learn to get in tune with your inner being. Some people even believed the place itself had mystical powers.

On the Tor – a hill above the town – was a ruined tower. From this vantage point you could survey the surrounding countryside. You could see the distant fields disappear into mist; the shapes of reservoirs and lakes; the outlines of farms, villages, solitary houses – the hems of other small country towns – spread out like garments on the land.

The Tor was the highest point for miles around. Once there had been a signal beacon there, its flames communicating uprisings or the deaths of kings. The rusted cradle had all but disintegrated and the crumbling tower was held together with modern steel, surrounded by a collar of scaffolding while workmen bolted it together to make sure it would last for another six hundred years.

Maybe the simple truth was that nowhere and nobody was ordinary; there was only the belief – the comforting illusion – that they were.

The morning assembly that day was solemn and bleak. Yesterday Jonah had just been long overdue; today he was confirmed missing. The headmaster stood up and made a short speech. 'We are all very concerned ... we all hope and pray ... if anyone here is able to give any information which might help in any way ... or if anybody thinks they might have seen something on Tuesday morning that they didn't mention before...'

Joe felt the flush of guilt again. Surely it must be obvious to everyone around him that he knew and was withholding something. People were putting their hands up, anxious to help or to at least appear helpful, possibly even seduced by the drama of it all and feeling that their hour had come.

'Please, sir, I think I maybe did see something funny now I think about it...'

'What was that, Michael?'

'Well ... I don't really remember now.'

'Well, when you do, come and tell us. As you can see, we have some police officers with us in assembly today, who will be setting up an incident room in my office temporarily. Some of you will have met them already, so there's no need to be nervous about talking.'

There were some detectives and two uniformed men, lurking at the back of the assembly hall. The detectives still looked like police officers, even in plain clothes; there were further, uniformed officers on duty outside the school.

When the headmaster had finished, he introduced the senior detective, a woman of about forty, who stood at the front and talked a while about the disappearance. She repeated the appeal for help while simultaneously trying to be reassuring. She told everyone to be careful, but didn't want to panic anyone. She seemed, at one moment, to be saying that there was no need to be concerned, and then that there was every need. But most of all, if anybody knew anything they hadn't previously revealed, then they ought to come forward as soon as possible, as any information would help and time was of the essence. There was no need to worry that anybody was going to get into any trouble. There were far more important things. The point was to find Jonah and to discover what had happened to him and to bring him home as soon as possible.

Yet still Joe held back. Reassurances were one thing, but could they be believed? And besides, what if Jonah was on his way back at this very moment – with a plausible story and good excuses that had nothing to do with fires and fire engines at all? Or what if he didn't actually *want* people looking for him – if he had plans and schemes of his own? No, when in doubt, say nothing.

Assembly broke up and people went to their classes. The atmosphere was solemn and downcast and remained so for the rest of the morning.

Joe resolved to give it until lunchtime. If Jonah hadn't turned up by then he'd tell them what he knew. Lunchtime. That gave Jonah a few extra hours to get home and to come up with his own explanations of why he'd stayed out for two whole nights and skived off school.

Lunchtime then. He'd give it till lunchtime, and then he'd spill the beans.

Chapter 3

The Truth

It didn't work out like that. When lunchtime came, Joe lost his nerve. He so much wanted to speak, but he couldn't do it. It would be impossible to admit the truth now without anger and recrimination – even punishment – descending on his head. He'd left it far too late. Jonah's gran would hate him, and his own mum too. Everybody would. They wouldn't understand. They wouldn't know about the value of a promise.

'Why didn't you say, Joe? Why didn't you tell us sooner?'

Precious, vital moments, as they said on the TV bulletins, were slipping – had already slipped – away. And it was Joe's fault.

The small town would soon be invaded by television crews and newspaper journalists, and everybody with a notebook would be looking for an interview, everybody with a microphone looking for somebody to speak into it, preferably someone who was related to or had known the vanished boy.

Why did they always do that? They homed in like heat-seeking missiles to the next of kin and then they stuck a microphone in your face and asked you how you felt. What were you supposed to say – that you were pleased, that you were happy? Wasn't it obvious that you were worried sick and the only reason you would talk to these vultures was in the hope that by doing so they might find the missing child for you. If you cooperated with them, they would cooperate with you in publicising the case.

They were ghouls. Didn't they have children of their own? Why did they need to ask how you felt? How would *they* have felt? How would anyone feel?

There were a few reporters there already, outside the school, taking shots of it, talking to parents, asking them if they had known the boy, whether their own children had been special friends with him? What kind of boy was he? What kind of town was this? It attracted a strange, drifting population, did it not, what with the festival and the mystical associations and the tower on top of the hill that people came from all over the world to see.

What business was it of anyone's? How was any of that going to help find Jonah?

Joe could see them out there, looking in through the fence as if the pupils in the school were like animals in a zoo. The children didn't like them there and some of the younger ones went back inside – though you weren't supposed to during lunch hour, not on fine days – and hid in the classrooms.

The police took charge of the situation and asked the reporters to back off as they were upsetting the children. They promised an official statement and a press conference at four o'clock in the headmaster's office. One reporter called after Mr Jeft, asking if he was doing anything to offer counselling services for the children who might be upset by the disappearance of their schoolmate and whether any of them – or even he himself – might be imagining the worst.

Counselling? He hadn't even thought of it. All he'd thought about was Jonah and what he could do to help find him. He talked to the deputy head, Mrs Tavistock, when he went back inside and asked if she could organise anything. She promised she would, so that anybody needing counselling would know where and when to find it.

Mr Jeft thought of cancelling the rest of the day's lessons and sending the children home. He consulted with the police, but they advised against it: the school should remain open, at least for the remainder of the day. To close it now would only make things seem even worse, not to mention the problem of contacting all the parents to ensure that they were able to pick up the children early, which would be an administrative nightmare in itself. The thing to do was to carry on as normal, even in the face of events such as this. You had to carry on with life, to make a show of coping with things and staying calm, if only for the children's sake.

Joe didn't eat any lunch. He couldn't have kept it down. He was afraid to say anything, and equally afraid not to. Fear and guilt balanced each other within him, like two monsters on a see-saw, and the result was that he was frozen, unable to move.

He kept telling himself that something would happen – some event, some sign – and then he would do it. But nothing did happen to make him go forward – or it did happen, but he still couldn't act.

I'll go when the dinner lady calls for the plates, he thought.

Her voice bellowed out, clear and loud, same as usual.

'Don't leave your dirty plates on the table, please! Put them in the rack!'

Still he didn't move. He couldn't do it. They'd be so angry now. They'd say he should never have left it so late, that so much valuable time had been lost, that if it hadn't been for him Jonah would have been home by now, safe and sound, with Elastoplast on the cuts or his arm in plaster or whatever the problem was.

He should have said straight away, right back when they'd first asked him about it, when they'd come to the house on the evening of Jonah's disappearance, when he'd lied and said he hadn't seen Jonah that morning at all.

I'll go when … I'll count to ten … count to ten and then I'll do it.

Ten. Twenty. Forty. Sixty. Seventy.

Still he didn't go.

He was alone in the dining room, the last to leave, his plate of food untouched before him, when Mrs Baddley, the dinner lady, came over. She saw his tears drop into his food, irrigating the mound of untouched mashed potato.

'You all right, love? Something the matter? Is it Jonah?'

He nodded.

'He was your friend, wasn't he?'

He nodded again. She found a tissue in the pocket of her apron and gave it to him. She was big and bulky and a little bit sweaty and smelt of dinners, but he was glad she was there. He was glad it was her and not Mr Grieves, the supply teacher with the short temper, or someone like that.

'You always sat together, didn't you? Here, you blow your nose.'

'Mrs Baddley…'

'What is it, love? Can't you eat your dinner? Would you like me to warm it up in the microwave? Be nice and hot in a couple of minutes.'

'Mrs Baddley … I saw him.'

She crouched down beside him now. She wasn't the dinner lady any more. She was somebody else, another parent with a child at the school.

'You saw him, love?'

Joe nodded. More tears fell. They landed on the sausages. Mrs Baddley moved his plate away.

'When was this?'

'Tuesday morning. I must have been the last to see him. He ran off after the fire engine. He wanted to see the fire.'

She reached up and moved her hair away from her eyes. She was wearing yellow rubber gloves, discoloured around the fingers.

'Did you not tell anyone, love?'

'No.'

She didn't ask him why. The silence said it all.

'I was afraid,' he said. 'I was scared.'

He began to sob pitifully now. She put her arm around his shoulders.

'What were you scared of?'

'Getting him –' his body shook, the words would hardly come – 'getting Jonah … into trouble. He made me promise when he ran off. He said promise not to tell and I did and…'

'I see. Don't worry now. It'll be all right.'

'Longer I left it … thought I'd get into trouble too … thought they'd think it was me…'

'No one thinks it's you, love.'

'Thought they'd say it was my fault for not saying sooner and that I'd get into trouble. But I didn't want *him* to get into trouble. That was why I didn't say. You see, Mrs Baddley?'

She crouched by him in the empty room. The other women were looking over from the serving hatch, wondering why the boy was so upset, and guessing that it was to do with the disappearance. No one was unaffected by it. Joe looked up at her. He tried to smile. She was all right really.

'You don't blame me, Mrs Baddley?'

'Of course I don't. I'd have been afraid too.'

'You would?'

''Course I would. And it shows qualities too … not saying

'Does it?'

'Yes. Loyalty to a friend. Not wanting to get him into trouble.'

'What should I do now?'

'Blow your nose.'

She found him another tissue and then, when he was ready, she stood up and put a comforting hand on his shoulder.

'I'll come with you. We'll go and see the headmaster, shall we?'

'You'll stay with me?'

'For a while. Till you tell me to go.'

She turned and yelled to the serving hatch.

'Lillian – clear up, would you? I've got to take him somewhere.'

They all watched as Joe got up. The clattering of plates and cutlery had fallen silent.

Joe left the table and they walked out of the dining room and into the corridor – the bulky dinner lady in her apron and the boy in his school sweatshirt and jeans. It seemed funny to have someone's hand on your shoulder when they had a big, yellow rubber glove on it.

As they approached the headmaster's office, she squeezed his arm, as if to say, 'It's all right now. You'll be OK.'

She knocked on the headmaster's door. He seemed surprised to see them. She explained what they had come for and he let them in. Several police officers were working in there; they looked up as he entered.

It wasn't as bad as he thought. The fear was always worse than the actuality. They were all understanding – or at least pretended to be – and nobody blamed him, or not to his face anyway, apart from his mother maybe, when she turned up. But even then all she said was, 'You should have told me, Joseph. You should have said.'

'I know, Mum. Sorry.'

'Well, you've said now. That's the main thing. Only how could you go so long, keeping that to yourself…'

He could tell that she'd have more to say about it when they got home – a lot more.

The police had taken Mr Jeft's office over completely, but he didn't seem to mind and he kept popping in every now and again, or sending Mrs Jeffreys, the secretary, in, to ask if anyone would like some tea.

'OK, Joseph, just tell us what happened.'

The detective taking his statement was the senior officer who had spoken at morning assembly. She said that he should call her Margaret.

'Right,' she said. 'So you *did* see Jonah on Tuesday morning after all?'

'We were walking to school,' he said.

'What time was this?'

'Usual time.'

'What time's the usual time?'

'Half-eight or so. You know.'

There was also another detective there, a young man of more junior rank, who asked the occasional question. But it wasn't like on the telly when there was one nasty police officer and one nice. They were both nice.

When his mum arrived, Mrs Baddley had slipped away.

'I'd better get back to the kitchen. Your mum's here now.'

Joe had nodded and thanked her for the tissue. He tried to smile at her as she left, but he was still crying a little. He wanted her to know that he was grateful and that she had made it easier. If it hadn't been for her, he might never have told anybody. It could have gone on for the rest of the day, or longer. Maybe forever. He might have taken it to his grave.

'So, half-eight or so, you say, Joe?'

'That's right. We were getting near the shop where we get stuff before school…'

He caught his mother's eye. She didn't know about that. She'd always assumed that the proper breakfast she gave him would be enough to take him through till lunchtime, that her good example had taught him not to bother with junk. But anyway, that didn't matter for now.

'So did you go into the shop?' the woman detective asked.

'Er … no.'

'Why was that?'

'The fire engine came by.'

'Right. The fire engine. And what did you do?'

'We stopped and looked at it and Jonah said – or maybe it was me said – one of us said, "There's the fire engine," and the other one said, "Yeah." And then one of us said, "There must be a fire," and then Jonah said, "Let's follow it." Then he started to run.'

The detective turned to her colleague. Even allowing for the seriousness of the situation, it was still somehow comic. The idea of this boy seeing a fire engine pass in the street and then deciding to run after it to see where it was going and to get a look at the fire.

'And what did you do?'

'I don't know. I mean … I ran a bit too … just because he'd started running and us being friends … I maybe felt I ought to follow him … keep him company.'

'How far did you get, Joe?'

'Not that far. Half a mile maybe. But you could see we'd never catch it. Or at least I could. But Jonah didn't, or he wouldn't believe it, and I think he yelled something about going home and getting our bikes, but I thought that was even dafter than running after it. By the time we'd got them it would be well and truly gone.'

'So then…?'

'I stopped running. I think I had a stitch. And I was worried about the time and being late for school, as I'm never late, not usually, though Jonah is sometimes.'

'Why's that? That he's late, but you're not, if you go to school together?'

'He goes wandering. Or he stands in the shop reading comics. He doesn't have the money to buy them. Not comics *and* sweets. So he buys sweets then stands reading the comics. Even when it's nearly time to go into school.'

'So what do you do?'

'I tell him I'm going and leave him there.'

'What happens?'

'He turns up in school five minutes later and if anybody notices he gets a telling-off. Sometimes they don't notice. He's only got his gran, you see. He hasn't got a mum and dad … well, he's got a dad, but he's miles away. He never sees him.'

'Yes, we know about Jonah's dad.'

Joe was conscious of his mother in the corner, stiffening slightly as she sat on her chair.

'Well … I don't have a dad either…' he went on. 'That is, I do, but he doesn't live with us…'

'Well, that's OK…'

It occurred to Joe for the first time ever that maybe that was part of the reason why he and Jonah had become friends – they had things in common. Neither of them had a father at home. Joe only had his mother; Jonah had his gran. It wasn't that anybody was unpleasant about it, or made remarks, and even if they had Mr Jeft wouldn't have tolerated it, for, as he was always saying, he wouldn't stand for that sort of thing and it just needed to be brought to his attention and he would soon stamp it out and come down on the culprits like a ton of bricks.

But there had never been any need for him to come down like a ton of bricks. Strange though, Joe thought now, that he had never before been consciously aware of the similarity of their predicaments. They were both only children too, without siblings. And that was what Jonah had been in a way – he had been his brother.

'So then, Joseph … look … I've drawn a little map here. Have a look at it, if you would. Now, following what you've told us … I've drawn you in here, near the shop at about half-past eight, would that be right?'

'About right, yes.'

'Then the fire engine passes…'

The woman turned to the young detective. She plainly outranked him. She was polite enough, but it was more of an order than a request.

'Brian, could you check with the fire station exactly what time they left?'

'Sure. I'll do it now.'

He went outside to use his mobile phone. As he went, a thought entered the woman's mind.

'Joseph … did Jonah have a phone?'

'At home?'

'No. A mobile. His gran says he didn't have one, but maybe he did and didn't tell her. Maybe he managed to buy one, or got one from his dad.'

'No.'

'You sure?'

'Sure. He didn't have one. If he did, he'd have given me his number.'

'OK. Never mind. So here's the map … the shop … the fire engine passes … goes in this direction … Jonah goes after it, you go after him … how far did you get before you turned back?'

'About there.'

'Round by the traffic lights?'

'Yeah. But it didn't stop for them.'

'And then?'

'I shouted to him to come back. I said it was stupid. I told him I wasn't coming – that I was going back to school before the bell went and we got into trouble.'

'What did he do?'

'Oh … you know … he was in one of his mad moods. He yelled something, only I didn't quite catch it. And then he was off again, haring after it. Looked like he was going to take a short cut.'

'Could you still see the fire engine at that point?'

'Not really. You could hear it though. You could hear it for ages.'

'And so he ran on after it?'

'Yeah. And … well … I do remember … the last thing he said. He said, "Don't tell anyone or I'll get into trouble." And he made me promise, see, not to tell on him. Then he said, "See ya later." Then he was gone. I promised, you see. I gave him my word not to tell anyone. I couldn't go back on a promise, could I? That would have been wrong.'

For the moment, the detective seemed to have run out of questions. Her colleague re-entered the room. He had some timings jotted down on a piece of paper. He handed it to her and she compared what was written there with the timings she had written on the map. They appeared to coincide.

'Thanks,' she said to him. Then she looked at Joe.

'Did I do the right thing?' Joe said. 'Telling … when he said not to tell?'

It was a breach of confidence and friendship, after all. Jonah had trusted him.

The detective took a moment to answer. 'You did the right thing … eventually,' she said. She might have added that Joe would have done an even righter thing if he had told somebody about this two days ago. The difference it could have made was the difference between life … and death.

But she didn't say any of that. The boy was still only a child after all, afraid and distressed, and who had tried, in his own way, to do the right thing by placing loyalty to his friend above everything. Admirable but misguided. She feared that the information had come too late to help find him. All it did was to point vaguely in the direction in which he might have gone.

As he left the room with his mother, Joe heard the policewoman ask the male officer, 'Did they say what the fire was? Whereabouts?'

'Just an exercise,' he said quietly, but still loud enough for Joe to overhear, 'in getting through the morning traffic. Just an exercise, that was all.'

There had been no fire. Jonah had run after it for nothing. All for nothing. No fire at all, not the slightest wisp of smoke, not a burning stack or a smouldering field, nothing. Just an exercise so that the crew could practise for the real thing.

It had all been another of Jonah's big illusions. He always wanted things to be exciting, that was the trouble. And because they often weren't, or not on a day-to-day basis anyway, he invented excitement for himself and for those around him. All the time.

'Look at that bloke, Langy,' Jonah might say. 'The tall one with the shoes. Looks like a criminal, don't you think?'

'Yeah. You're right, he does.'

(Joe didn't think the man looked remotely like a criminal. But he went along with it. Why not? What else was there to do?)

'Let's follow him, see what he's up to.'

'Right.'

So they would follow the man, or whoever it was who had aroused Jonah's suspicions that day. But he would only turn out to be on his way to the hardware store, or getting his car out of the car park, or meeting his wife outside the supermarket.

It was ludicrous, always had been, and the most ludicrous thing about it had been how willingly Joe had gone along with it all. He had been an enthusiastic participant in Jonah's world of fantasies and dreams; his world of Mr Bigs and criminal masterminds, with plans for world domination and explosives inside their shoes.

He had gone along with it principally because it was better than reality. Jonah's world always had been. It had been far-fetched, eccentric, a dramatic world full of spies and plots, kidnaps and bank robberies and dramatic goings-on.

Only the thing was that now it looked as if Jonah's vision of the world had been right after all, for he had vanished off the face of the earth into some extraordinary mystery.

So maybe that was where Jonah had gone – into the world he had created for himself. Into his own imagination. Perhaps that was where he was now, inside his own mind. But where was his mind? You needed a brain for a mind and a brain needed a body.

'Don't worry, son …' the detective said.

Joe turned to look back at her from the doorway of the headmaster's office.

'Don't worry,' she said again, trying to be kind and friendly and reassuring. 'It wasn't your fault.'

Joe nodded mutely.

'We'll find your friend.'

Joe looked into the policewoman's eyes and saw the doubt that her words were trying both to conceal and to dispel.

You won't, you know. You'll never find him. He's gone forever. And it is my fault.

The words rose in his throat, but he swallowed them back down again. He didn't want to think them, let alone say them; they seemed like such an enormous betrayal, not just of Jonah, but of hope. But he knew that they were true. He knew it from the coldness of his own skin and the dryness of his mouth and the lump in his stomach like a lead weight.

He nodded and left the room, his mother beside him.

Couldn't they see it? Could none of them see what Joe sensed so clearly? They were not going to find him. Jonah was not coming back. He had vanished forever, like the children who had followed the Piper of Hamelin, who had entered the darkness of the cave, and the rocks had closed behind them.

He left the school building and walked across the playground, his mother keeping close to him. They walked in near silence all the way home. The very town itself seemed muffled, as if people were walking with rags tied around their shoes. It was as if snow had fallen, and yet the sun was shining and the sky was clear.

'They'll find him, Joe, they'll find him,' his mother said.

How funny it was, the way they went on reassuring you, as if the mere repetition of promises gave them the power to make them come true. He stopped and turned and looked up at her face. He shook his head.

'They won't, Mum. He's gone forever. There's only one person in the world who can find him, and right now even he can't do that.'

'Who, Joe? Who can find him?'

'Me,' he said. 'I'm the only one. I lost him … I left it too late … I didn't tell anyone … so I have to find him now.'

He saw from her eyes that she was deliberately not saying things that she could have said, that she was making allowances and considering the circumstances and realising that he had had a very bad shock and she didn't want to upset him further.

'Well … let's hope someone finds him … very soon.'

'There's only me can do it, Mum,' Joe said. 'One day I'll know … one day it will come … and I'll know then where he's gone.'

He walked on, a few steps in front of her, his eyes on the ground, his hands thrust deep into his pockets. He didn't want to tell her the rest, because he knew it would have upset her too much, but it was the truth just the same and it filled him with fear.

To find out where Jonah had gone, he would have to go there too. One day it would come. He would hear something or see something, and he would know that this was the day. It might be only hours from now, it might be years. But he would know it when it came. It might be a siren in the street, or a shooting star in the sky, but he would run after it just as Jonah had run after it, and he would vanish too, just as Jonah had. And then, he knew, he would find him.

But in doing so, he would risk losing everything – everything and everyone he loved. He might even risk far more than that. He might lose life itself.

Chapter 4

Re-enactment

'Can we come in?'

It was the same detective as before, the one from the school. She had a junior officer with her, only this time it was a different one. Joe had seen them arriving from his bedroom window. They had parked the police car right outside the house.

'Joseph! Joe!'

He hurried down the stairs at the sound of his mother's voice. They were all in the kitchen, sitting around the stripped-pine table that his mother had rescued from a junk shop. She was quite good at stuff like that – shopping for bargains and making do. She could stretch a five-pound note like a piece of elastic. But maybe she had to be good at making do, for she was so bad at making money. Just as long as you were good at making money, Joe sometimes thought, you could be terrible at everything else.

'Joseph…'

'Hi.'

'We've come to ask you a favour. There's a way you could help us.'

'How's that?'

'Well, we've put an appeal out, as you know, for people who might have seen him … who might have seen anything at all, no matter how unremarkable … to come forward and let us know.'

'Right.'

'It was on the TV earlier.'

'Yeah, I saw it.'

'We were watching the news,' his mother explained, somewhat unnecessarily, Joe thought.

'The thing is, Joe, sometimes people don't remember. They don't really know what they've seen half the time. We all do it. You know – you go to school, you pass a hundred people but you don't really notice them or remember their faces. There could be all sorts of things going on, but you don't necessarily remember, and yet, you know, it's a funny thing, but quite often it's still in there, in your head. Things you've seen but didn't really notice. They're still there in your memory, and sometimes all it needs is a little nudge to help you remember them again.'

'Yeah?'

The detective looked at Mrs Langley and then down at her hands.

'We'd like to reconstruct … re-enact … what happened last Tuesday morning. We'd like you to retrace his steps.'

'To be Jonah?'

'That's right, yes. We'd like you to go out tomorrow morning … same time, taking the same route, wearing the same clothes … and then, what we're going to do is arrange with the fire brigade for one of the fire engines to go past at roughly the same time. We want people to watch and to think back – to see if there's something they saw but overlooked.'

'Some kind of clue, you mean?'

'That's right.'

'And you want me to be Jonah?'

The detective cleared her throat. She glanced at Joe's mother again. She was a bit of a hippy type and the detective wasn't quite sure how to deal with her, where she stood on her view of the police. She probably called them 'fuzz' or 'pigs' without even thinking about it.

'Only if you feel … and if your mother feels … We could use an actor…'

'No, I'll do it,' Joe said.

'You don't have to, Joseph,' his mother said protectively. 'Not if it's too upsetting. I'm sure they could find another boy…'

'Of course, of course.' The detective nodded. 'Absolutely no pressure. It's just that…'

'That as I was with him I'd know. I'd know what he did better than anyone?'

'That's right.'

Joe knew that his mother was trying to look at him and to give him some kind of message with her eyes, but he deliberately failed to make contact.

'I'll do it, that's OK.'

'Just wear your school uniform and retrace your steps.'

'OK.'

'We'll be with you, keeping an eye on you. Not too near, but we'll be there.'

'OK. And what happens when I hear the siren?'

'Just do what he did.'

'Run?'

'Yes … I mean … it doesn't have to be fast or far … just run a little way, in the direction he took, and then when you feel you've gone as far as you can usefully go, just stop.'

'All right.'

'Good. And to make it really helpful, we'd like some television cameras to be there, following what you're doing. OK?'

'OK.'

'You're happy to do that?'

He nodded. 'If it helps find Jonah,' he made himself say, though he knew that it wouldn't.

The two police officers seemed genuinely grateful and relieved. They sat back in their chairs, more relaxed now, and accepted the offer of some tea.

'It'll really help us, Joseph,' the detective said. 'People often think it doesn't, but it does, an awful lot. It's amazing what people can recall when you jog their memories. They suddenly recollect something they've seen – a van, a car, someone acting suspiciously.'

'Sugar?' Joe's mum asked.

He watched as his mother poured tea into the mugs that she had made herself at her pottery classes. They were unglazed and he hated the feel of the clay against his lips. He always avoided drinking from them if he could.

'Would you like some milk, Joe?'

'It's all right, I'll get it.'

He fetched some milk from the fridge, pouring it into a tumbler before his mother could put it into a mug.

'OK. Well, we'll put it out on the news bulletin tonight,' the detective said, 'that we're going to reconstruct the journey in the morning, and we'll ask people to watch and see if it helps them remember.'

'What shall I do?' Joe asked. 'Shall I just set off, usual time?'

The woman smiled.

'No. We'll come for you. About eight-fifteen? Eight-ten? That should be early enough.'

'All right.'

'You'll be ready then?'

His mother answered for him.

'We'll be ready.'

'Wear exactly what Jonah was wearing – your school uniform. And remember your backpack.'

'Right.'

The detective paused a moment, as if she had previously omitted to ask him something and now was the time to do it.

'Tell me, Joe, what did Jonah do with his backpack? We know he had it with him when he left home. What did he do with it when he started to run after the fire engine? Did he give it to you? Did he dump it? What?'

'No, he kept it with him and went on running.'

'Wouldn't that have been uncomfortable? Didn't it slow him down?'

'Not that you'd notice. There was nothing much in it anyway. I mean, it wasn't a games day and he didn't take packed lunches. He has school dinners, same as I do. He sits next to me. So there was nothing in it really – maybe a couple of books and that was it.'

'OK. You didn't have a lot of homework the night before or anything?'

'No. So you want me to bring my backpack then, in the morning?'

'Yes. Yours is the same as his – right?'

Joe hesitated a moment before answering.

'Yeah, we had the same,' he said. 'Identical.'

The detectives finished their tea and got up.

'Well, thank you, Joe, thank you, Mrs Langley.'

They saw them to the door.

'Any news at all?' Joe's mum asked.

The detective looked grim-faced and shook her head.

'How's his grandmother? Can I do anything?' she offered.

'She's being taken care of,' the detective said. 'Thanks all the same.'

'How's she taking it?'

Mum, Joe thought, do you have to say things like that?

'Badly, as you'd expect.'

'Well, if there's anything else we can do.'

'No, that's fine for now. We'll see you in the morning then, Joe. And thanks, thanks again. See you get a good night's sleep now.'

Then they were gone and his mother was closing the door and, unusually for her, double-locking and then bolting it, as if there were child-stealers out there who might be looking to break in.

Too late, Mum, Joe thought. People always lock their doors too late – after things have happened, not before. They only learn to lock their doors when there's no longer any point.

'Better get a good night's sleep now then, Joseph, like the policewoman said.'

Yeah, Mum, I heard her.

'Going to go up and brush your teeth?'

'In a minute. Can I see the TV first?'

They watched the news again. There were pictures of the searchers, the police and volunteers, going over the fields and through the ditches. Arc lights were being set up so that the search could continue throughout the night. They were all there – police, local townspeople, the travellers – working shoulder to shoulder with the farmers and shepherds and cowmen and labourers who could take a few hours from their work on the land or until the next milking. They searched in the brambles and the undergrowth, looking for any sign at all, for a thread, a button, a lace, a footprint, a fragment of cloth.

The great sun was dipping down. The Tor was visible with the ruined tower on its top, looking eerie in the purple twilight. Beneath the Tor the Levels stretched on for mile after mile. The irrigation channels gleamed like silver pencilled lines drawn with the aid of a ruler in the green of the fields. Swans sat at the field-sides, or struggled to rise into the sky with the sound of whining wings. A heron or two, long-legged and snooty, half ran, half flew over the ploughed ruts of earth. And there, along the roadside, were the cropped willow trees, pollarded and hacked, with nothing left but carbuncles and fists where their branches should have been. They looked as if they had tumours.

The men – and they were all men – bowed down over the earth and went on looking for some trace of the vanished boy. One of them stood up, his hand at the small of his back, pausing a moment to let the stiffness go away. As he did so, a heron took off from an adjacent field and rose elegantly into the sky. It flew on, over the fields and the peat workings where the bulldozers had cut deep brown scars into the land. Next to the scars were little hills and mini-mountains of peat, ready for bagging up for transportation and for resale at the garden centres.

Maybe he flew away, the man thought, just flew away. It's like he took off, into the sky.

For a moment he had an image of a flying boy, gliding like the heron into the twilight. He held his hand to his eyes and watched until he could see the heron no longer. Where had it gone? You couldn't see it, but it was still there, still alive somewhere.

Then a generator throbbed into life and its sound broke the silence just as the arc lights broke the gathering darkness.

The man resumed his searching, parting the grass, looking for something, anything.

It was like it was your own really – your very own son.

Chapter 5

The Alley

Joe woke a few times in the night, in anticipation of the morning, fearing that he had overslept and it was already too late. He grabbed at the clock in the semi-darkness, managing to knock it over. The back came off and the battery fell out, so then he had to put the light on and find the pieces and reassemble the thing and reset the alarm. No sooner had he got back to sleep than his mother was tapping at the bedroom door.

'Joseph … Joseph … it's seven-thirty now. Time to get up. They'll be here soon.'

In truth, they were already outside, sitting waiting in their cars, sipping steaming coffee that left condensation on the windscreen. It was nearly a week now since Jonah had vanished. The police team had questioned friends, neighbours, relatives, passers-by, total strangers and listed offenders for miles around; they had followed every single lead, but had come up with nothing. Jonah's grandmother had gone to stay with a relative; she didn't seem able to take it all in, and kept asking where he had gone to and what time he would be expected back.

One or two witnesses had remembered the fire engine and the boy running, but then he had simply vanished. One elderly woman who had been on her way to the minimart said that she thought she might have seen an unfamiliar van, battered and dented and more rust than white. It was something to go on, but had produced nothing substantial so far. The world was full of white battered vans, and she had no idea as to its make or number plate, or even which direction it had been travelling in or precisely when she had seen it.

Joe came downstairs and ate breakfast. It was muesli, the one with nothing artificial added and no extra sugar. It was all right, he didn't mind it – he just wished sometimes that his mother would buy something else, some junk, just once in a while for the heck of it, some full-fat, sugar-laden, honey-coated, brimful-of-additives junk.

He went up to brush his teeth. While he was in the bathroom the bell rang and his mother let the police in. He spat out into the sink and went back down.

'Morning, Joe…'

'Hi.'

'You OK?'

'I'm fine.'

It was one of the policemen who had been at the school, the young one with the fair hair and blue eyes. He was pleasant enough; they all were. The senior detective was outside, talking into a mobile phone.

'No need to go just yet. In a minute or two,' the policeman said.

'OK, I'll just get my bag.'

Joe got the backpack and put a few things in it, so that it would be more or less the same as Jonah's had been. They'd both got them round about the same time. It was a choice of Nike or another one and they both ended up with Nike.

'OK. There's some TV people outside who will be following you, Joe, but just ignore them as much as you can. Try to pretend they're not there. It's just another ordinary day and you're on your way to school. Imagine Jonah's with you and you're walking along. And then, try to do what he did … when you hear the siren … OK?'

'OK.'

There was tension and fear in his stomach again. He felt heavy, awkward and self-conscious; he was afraid that he would do something wrong while everybody was watching. Maybe he would trip up or embarrass himself somehow. He was even afraid that he might need to go to the toilet.

'OK, I think it's time now, if you're ready, Joe?'

'OK, I'm ready. Mum…'

'I'll see you in a little while. Or would you rather I came along…?'

'Don't worry, I don't think that will be necessary, Mrs Langley, unless Joe would prefer…'

He shook his head. He preferred to manage without her. She'd make him self-conscious if she were there.

'We'll bring him right back.'

Joe looked up, surprised.

'Won't I be going to school after?'

His mother shook her head.

'School's closed today.'

'Why?'

But it was obvious why. Nobody answered the question; the look on Joe's face was enough to tell them that he had answered it for himself.

They left the house.

'OK, Joe. In your own time now. Walk along past Jonah's house and then to where the crossing is. Take your usual route. The fire engine's waiting around a corner. It'll start up when I radio them that you're on your way and getting near.'

'And when I hear the siren should I start running?'

'Just do what Jonah did, as far as you can remember.'

'When do I stop running? How far shall I go? He took a short cut, see, down the back way. I don't know exactly where he went. I can only go so far.'

'Just go as far as you can then, as far as you recall seeing him go or, if anything comes to you, go with it. We'll be with you.'

'OK.'

He shouldered his backpack, thrust his hands into his pockets and started walking.

They followed behind him, the camera crews and the police. He walked on, stiff and self-conscious, but trying to act naturally and to seem relaxed.

He took the usual route. People turned to look at him; they stopped their journeys to watch; they lined the pavements and gathered in the shop doorways; the shopkeepers and counter assistants came out to see him pass. Cars pulled up at the roadside and the drivers shut off their engines. A silence fell over the town.

On he walked. There was Jonah, a picture in his mind; he could see him turning out of the pathway and waiting for Joe to catch up so that they could walk to school together.

'Hi, Jonah.'

'Hi, Langy, mate.'

'See any telly last night?'

'Not much. You?'

'No. My mum only lets me see an hour. Though she always stays up watching it.'

'Going to the shop?'

'All right.'

He walked on, pretending it was last week – that fateful Tuesday when they had gone into the shop together, him and Jonah. They'd gone and bought sweets. He'd said they hadn't, but they had really. He'd lied because his mother was listening and he didn't want her to know.

But now Joe walked into the shop – the re-enactment had to be done properly. The newsagent was standing outside on the pavement, watching. He stood aside to let Joe enter, then followed him inside to serve him. Joe bought some snacks – junk food his mother wouldn't have approved of, especially not between meals and straight after breakfast. He came out, breaking one of the chocolate bars in half. Half each, that was the way.

Where was Jonah? Yes, there he was. He could see him again in his mind's eye, hear his own voice talking to him, saying, *'Here you are, mate. Swap you a bit,'* as they divided their purchases between them.

He'd have given him all of it if Jonah had been there now. He didn't feel like eating, not this morning. He put the bar into his pocket and went on his way. Everyone around was looking now, they all seemed to know, everyone in the street. This was how it had happened, this had been the boy.

He was nearing the road crossing. He was conscious of the TV cameras following him. He could hear one of the policemen behind him talking into his radio. 'He's approaching now, if you could start up and get moving.' Next he heard the siren of the fire engine. Faint at first, then gathering volume.

'Come on! Let's follow it! Let's find the fire!' the voice called from inside his brain.

'No, no, we'll be late for school! Come back!'

But he had to follow this time. He was Jonah now and he had to do what Jonah had done. He felt it now as Jonah must have – the fire was irresistible. He felt no fear. It was liberating in a way, he just didn't care, not about missing school or getting into trouble. He just wanted to run after the fire.

There was the engine now, heading away down the street, the driver grim-faced, the other men crowded into the cab or holding on to the grab-rails; their eyes all turned to see the boy this time. None of them had noticed him before, not the first time round.

Then he ran. He was after it now. He felt the excitement, just as Jonah must have done – the rush, the kick inside. He forgot about the rest of them, the cameras, the people behind, even why he was there. He just ran, letting his feet carry him off in the direction of the siren and the engine, already disappearing out of sight.

He ran, faster than ever, just as Jonah had run. He passed the point at which Jonah had briefly stopped and called back to him and had made him promise not to tell where he had gone. Then he ran on again, on and on.

He didn't even need to think where to go. His feet were leading him, Jonah was taking him; he had left some invisible track in the road and Joe's feet could follow it blindly. He could hear the people running behind him, some of them sounding heavy-footed and out of breath – maybe an overweight cameraman struggling with equipment.

'Down here, Langy. This way. Follow me. Go the way I went.'

He made a sudden turn, down a narrow, unfamiliar alley. He had lived in this town a long time and had never once noticed it before. It was no wider than a man with outstretched arms. He ran on down it, through the gloom of the overhanging rooftops and the damp of the puddles.

Jonah had come this way.

He'd left a trail. Joe knew he had, as surely as a wild animal leaves a spoor, like a cat leaves fur on a barbed-wire fence…

'Jonah!'

It was his own voice, shouting Jonah's name. Maybe he was there. Maybe it was today he would find him, down at the end of the alley. He hadn't expected it to be so soon.

He came to the end and stopped.

Silence. No footsteps following. Nobody behind him any more. Where were they? Where had they gone? The police, the TV crews?

He'd lost them. He'd swerved into the alley and they hadn't seen where he had gone. He was all alone, maybe just as Jonah had been. He could still hear the siren, faint in the distance, far, far away.

Which way now?

'Jonah! Jonah! Are you there?'

His voice called back to him, echoing from the empty alley. He turned to the left, feeling Jonah had gone this way, but no longer sure. He jogged on alone along a narrow street. As he came to the end of it, he saw that there was a van parked there. Its door was open, half blocking the pavement. There seemed to be a figure inside, in the front of the van, but there was nobody else around. The street was so narrow that it was impossible to pass the van on the other side. He had to walk past the open door or turn around and go back.

The van was white, with spots of rust on it. There were dents in the rear door and the wings.

He slowed down. He could see a man's eyes now, looking at him from the rear-view mirror.

What should he do? If he went back he felt that it would be over, he would never find Jonah, not ever. But if he went on ... if he tried to squeeze between the open door and the wall...

He stopped. There was movement from within the van. The man got out. He was dressed in blue overalls. He was middle-aged, overweight, with thinning hair. There were tattoos on his hands. He looked fat, but strong, as if most of him were muscle. He stood by the open door. Joe looked up at him; his heart was thudding in his chest.

Then the man smiled.

'Sorry, son. Did you want to get past?'

He half closed the door to make room for Joe to get by.

'Sorry. I'm blocking the way. I'll be gone in a minute. Just finishing off a job. Come on. Here you go. You'll get by.'

He wanted to turn and run back, but Jonah wouldn't let him. If he went back now Jonah would be lost forever. He had to go forward – it was a test almost; an article of faith.

'Thanks.'

He walked ahead. The man squeezed in. Joe was level with him. If it were going to happen, it would happen now.

'You OK there?'

'Thanks.'

'Mind how you go.'

He was past. And nothing had happened. He looked back. The man seemed different now. He was ruddy-faced and jovial. He had a sandwich in his hand and he was tucking into it, munching away. Then another man appeared from a nearby building, carrying a ladder and a couple of planks. He threw the stuff into the rear of the van and the engine started up.

Joe came to an intersection. The van drove out and passed him, and the driver gave him a wave.

Which way now, Jonah? To the Five Ways roundabout and the road out of town? Past the Tor and out towards the Levels? Was this the way you came?

He jogged on, but the trail that he had felt so keenly was cooling. Then it went cold. He stopped and stood looking around him. The town was behind him, the open fields were ahead. There was nowhere that Jonah could have gone except out into the countryside. Something important and significant had happened right here, Joe just knew it – some event, some decision.

'Joseph!'

It was his mother. Some police cars swept up and she was in one of them; she had followed him after all. She was almost hysterical, opening the door before the car had stopped properly and running to scoop him up in her arms.

'Joseph! Joseph! We lost you! What happened to you? Where did you go? You were there one second and…'

The policeman was there too.

'God, but you had me worried, son. I'm sorry, Mrs Langley, so sorry.'

'How could you have lost him? How *could* you!'

'I'm so sorry. But he's all right now, aren't you, Joe? Nothing happened. You're all right?'

Joe suffered his mother's embraces and tears. But he couldn't respond to them. He had something important to say.

'Excuse me…'

'Yes?' The policeman was on his way back to the car to make a radio call.

'This is where it happened,' Joe said. 'Right on this spot, where I'm standing. He made a decision. He was going to turn back but he didn't. This was it – the point of no return.'

Joe's mother had calmed down. She looked from him to the policeman.

'How do you know, Joseph?'

'I just know,' he said. 'He was my friend and I just know. It was on this spot. If he'd turned back here, he'd have been all right. Afterwards, it was too late.'

The policeman looked at Joe strangely then called to his colleague in the car.

'Would you bring some chalk?'

When it came he drew a ring on the tarmac around Joe's feet. He couldn't rightly have said why he did it. It wasn't just to humour the boy, it was more than that – to show some respect for him, that he was taken seriously.

When the circle was complete, Joe stepped from it. He looked at it and nodded his head. They had marked it, the final point of possible return. Then he looked up.

'Did it do any good? The reconstruction?'

'Might have done. Too soon to say. We'll have to see if it's jogged any memories. We'll know when the phones start ringing. But you had us worried, Joe. How did you disappear like that? One second you were there, the next you weren't.'

'I went down the alley.'

'What alley?'

'The one … you know…'

'No. I don't. Get in the car and show us.'

They drove all around but he couldn't find it again. There was an alley, but it didn't look right somehow, it seemed different, like it was the wrong one. Or maybe that was just his changed perspective; maybe perception depended on urgency and mood.

It reminded him of the Pied Piper again, who had led all the children into a cave in the rock, but the entrance had closed behind them and was never found.

The police dropped Joe and his mother back home. He wished that they hadn't closed the school. He'd have to spend all day with his mother now and there wasn't really anything for him to do. He'd have to go with her to the shop where she worked every afternoon, the one that sold all the mystical stuff, the one with the dreamcatchers and the Buddhas and the joss sticks in the window. He'd be bored out of his mind.

Maybe I could see a friend, he thought. The words were almost out of his mouth before he realised that Jonah was really the only friend he had had, the only special friend, not just a schoolmate or an acquaintance or someone on the football team, but a real friend – someone who understood. His mother had read him a quotation once. 'A friend is another self,' she had read. And maybe it was.

He didn't have anyone now, not really.

He sat in the kitchen and felt suddenly lonely. Even though his mother was there and he wasn't alone, he still felt that way. He felt that they were both lonely, because there was only them, and they weren't part of anything larger.

'There's just us, really, isn't there, Mum?'

'What do you mean?'

'Oh … nothing. I don't know. I don't have any friends any more, Mum.'

'Yes you do. Of course you do. You have lots of them. Everyone in your class.'

He shook his head, not sadly, not self-pityingly, just stating the facts.

'I don't, Mum. Not any more. I've lost him, now. My friend has gone.'

His mother reached out and took him, big as he was, on to her knee. She held him as he wept, as he snuggled into her, feeling the texture of crushed velvet, smelling her scent of musk and patchouli oil. When he'd stopped crying, she made them a lunch of hummus-and-salad sandwiches on wholemeal bread. They didn't eat meat, either of them. They both felt, for moral reasons, that it was wrong to kill things. Of course, not everybody in the world felt that way. Other people had other views. But everyone was entitled to their own opinion.

Chapter 6

The Days

More than anything now, what he felt was anger. Anger towards all those who suddenly appeared, claiming grief and distress and saying how they missed Jonah terribly and how he had always been their best friend. Agatha, who always had leading roles in the school plays, turned up one night on the television with damp eyes and a handkerchief in her hand, saying that it had been very hard for all of them, but at least she personally was making a little progress, thanks to the counselling, and that it was the relatives her heart went out to more than anyone, and everyone was remembering them in their prayers.

The whole thing was nothing but a performance.

It made him feel cold inside, all these people who suddenly claimed grief and lifelong friendship; people who had barely been on nodding terms with Jonah, some who had even actively disliked him. They were all Jonah's best friends now and available for interview, willing – anxious even – to display the contents of their hearts.

'She never liked him!' he said angrily to his mother. 'She never even talked to him half the time. And if he ever got an answer wrong in class or something, she'd sit there and roll her eyes.'

They were cashing in, that was all. It filled him with cold fury that anyone could do that – grasp any opportunity to put themselves in the spotlight and make themselves the centre of attention. It was Jonah who was important, not them. Who wanted to know what they thought or felt about it? Who were they to claim intimacy and friendship with somebody they had, at best, been indifferent to or had completely ignored or had regarded as the class head case? All of them knew that Joe had really been Jonah's best friend. They treated him with kid gloves now. They were wary – they didn't know what to say to him.

In the second week after Jonah had disappeared, his father finally turned up, saying he had been abroad, working on a building job in Spain, and had only just heard about what had happened. Jonah's mother had died when he was still a baby, and his father had taken off soon after, leaving Jonah with his dead wife's mother – Jonah's gran. He was back now though, like the proverbial bad penny, turning up just when you thought you'd seen the last of him forever. Not once, in the years that they had known each other, had Joe ever heard Jonah say that his father had been to see him or had sent him a present on his birthday, or even a card.

So the sudden and emotional appearance of Jonah's father made him angry too. There he was on the television, making a moving appeal for any information that might lead to Jonah's return. He asked, he pleaded, for anyone who may have seen anything or who might know anything to come forward. He broke down at one point and, although the programme makers could easily have cut away from him then, they didn't – they just let the camera dwell on him, knowing this was good television, with plenty of impact for the viewers.

After the appeal, he was interviewed by one of the newspapers. Joe's mother bought it and left it lying around. There was a picture of him, stern-faced and angry, thumping his fist into his other hand. He was quoted as saying that, when the police found whoever it was who had taken Jonah, then he personally would like to have just five minutes alone with them, and that they ought to bring back the death penalty for people like that, though, in his view, hanging was too good for them.

But all Joe could think was that this was the man who hadn't been able to spare five minutes of his time for his own son – not for years. It was all well and good for him to be angry now and to go around telling everyone how much he had loved Jonah, but where had he been when he could have done something? Did it not cross his mind that if he had been there, at home with him, then perhaps none of this would have happened?

If it did occur to him, he didn't show it. He just came across as a self-centred, angry man, concerned more with his own reactions to the loss of his son than with the loss itself. He even seemed to be enjoying his moment of attention. For the first time in his life people were ready to listen to what he had to say. At last his opinions mattered; he was important.

He went on at length about 'people like that'. Only who exactly, Joe wondered, were 'people like that'? He asked his mother, but she didn't really define it. She just said, 'Bad people. People who do bad things.'

In all honesty, Joe thought that Jonah's father looked a bit 'people like that' himself, though he would never have said so, least of all to him. The man's attitude made Joe want to hit him.

The police continued diligently with their hunt for Jonah, widening their searches of parks, forestry and farmland. They dredged canals and sent divers into the rivers. They made house-to-house enquiries and looked in every shed, outhouse and barn for miles around. They interviewed several men – even took some of them in for questioning and kept them in custody overnight. These were people with criminal records, believed capable of abduction. They were all later released without charge. They had no connection with the incident or, if they did, it could not be proved.

On the twelfth day after Jonah's disappearance, his gran suffered a stroke. It happened as she was drinking a cup of tea. The cup fell from her hand, spilling the lukewarm, milky tea over her dress. She was taken to hospital but she never regained consciousness. She died three days later. In some ways – some said – it was a merciful release. To have to live without Jonah, never knowing what had happened to him, would have been too much for her to bear.

So the days turned into weeks, and the weeks into months. At first the police were positive they would find him, then their words grew less confident and more circumspect. They were 'still following every lead' and they would 'never give up on the case'. There were front-page photographs of Jonah in the newspapers, his portrait clipped from the class photos and placed underneath the headline Where Is He? But no answer to the question ever came.

At length, the number of officers investigating the case was reduced. Five months had gone by and not a single lead had brought anything useful or substantial. Jonah had simply gone, evaporated from the face of the earth like rising mist in morning sunlight.

'Cases like this are never closed and will remain open indefinitely until such time as further information becomes available.'

It was the official way of saying that they had given up and yet they had not given up. Or rather it wasn't so much that they had given up, more that they had looked everywhere, tried everything and there was simply nothing else that they could do or, if there was, they didn't know what. They could only wait.

It was like a conjuring trick, Joe thought. You saw something disappear before your very eyes, yet you knew that it hadn't really, for that defied the laws of physics and nature. You couldn't explain it – yet there had to be an explanation. And this was the same. There was an explanation, but it wasn't one that ordinary means could provide.

The police tried the magicians too. Quietly, that was, in confidence, not really expecting much, just feeling that they could leave no avenue unexplored, no offer of help turned down.

They were in the right place for it. The town was full of amiable and mainly harmless people who believed themselves gifted with mystical powers, second sight and psychic abilities. It was why they had gravitated towards the area in the first place. Several of them came forward, offering their services to help find the vanished boy. Some had had visions, some had had dreams. Someone had seen him running over a field through the vivid yellow of a crop of oilseed flowers; another knew just where he was buried and told the police exactly where to dig. So they dug and found nothing, just an old iron pickaxe head and some lumps of stone.

The months went by. Time diluted the strength of people's feelings. Urgency gave way to desperation, which in turn gave way to resignation. Nobody said as much, but they all accepted that he would never now be found or, if he was, he would not be alive. Only Joe went on believing otherwise. He knew that Jonah was still alive. Or maybe he only knew it because he wanted it that way. He alone refused to accept the possibility that Jonah would never be found.

Even when Jonah's clothes turned up. It wasn't all of them, just his sweatshirt. And it was not discovered locally, but on a beach up in the north, miles and miles away. It was there, lying by a rock, weighted down with a stone. Jonah's name was in it, where his gran had sewn in the nametape. The sweatshirt was sodden from the seawater. The police scientists did all sorts of forensic tests on it, but none of them helped. Time and salt had eroded whatever clues it might have supplied. A second investigation was opened in the surrounding area, but that too petered out eventually. They sent divers into the cold, clear seawater – they found nothing.

All the signs were that Jonah would not be coming back. But Joe was neither sensible nor realistic, and he just went on believing. Belief transcended both sense and reason. In some ways Joe felt that it was only his faith in Jonah's continuing existence that was keeping him alive. Wherever he was, whatever he was doing, he had Joe Langley to believe in him. If Joe ever began to doubt, then Jonah would be gone. And that simply could not be allowed to happen. Ever.

For a long time parents stopped their children going anywhere. If they did, then they had to go in pairs or groups. Lightning is not supposed to strike twice in the same place, but the lightning might not know that and might miscalculate, so nobody was relying on it and they preferred to take their own precautions, however late or unnecessary they now were.

It was a good six months to a year before the sense of imminent danger began to wear off. People eventually started to relax and to allow their children to be alone again and to learn independence, without going into an instant panic when they were more than five minutes late.

Finally, almost a year after Jonah's disappearance, Joe's mother agreed that he could go on bike rides again. He'd gone on them with Jonah in the past, but now he went alone. The roads around the Levels were quiet, with not much traffic on them. He always had to say where he was going and when he would be back, and to take his mobile phone.

It was easy riding, mostly, as there weren't many steep hills at all. The Tor was the steepest and the Levels were pancake flat. Once, so the local history guide said, they had been under water and the Tor had been an island in a brackish sea, but then the climate and the topography had changed. The Levels still flooded sometimes, in the heavy winter rain. They lay half submerged then, with the sheep gathered in huddled circles upon what remained of dry land in the centre of the fields, baaing and complaining as the farmer rowed towards them in his flat wooden boat or drove his high-wheeled tractor through the squelching mud.

Joe didn't know how many miles he rode, for he only counted time, not distance, and he only counted time so as not to be late home. Distance was irrelevant to him; he got no satisfaction from cycling a little further this week than last. It wasn't the distance. That wasn't the point. It was just being there, that was what he enjoyed – the speed, the motion, the play of the shadows, the wheels spinning on the long, straight road.

There had been no music festival the year Jonah disappeared, though there was one scheduled for this year. It was too much trouble to organise on an annual basis, and the locals wouldn't have liked it. Once every two years was just about fine. It was only one weekend in summer but it was a lot of disruption just the same. On the other hand, the thousands of visitors brought hundreds of thousands of pounds with them, a lot of which found its way into the local shops. But there was always trouble too, of one kind or another, and some of the people who came for the festival took months to go home, or never went home at all.

Joe rode out every weekend, whenever it was dry. It didn't have to be sunny or warm, just as long as he didn't get soaked. He took a different direction every weekend, exploring at first and then retracing favourite routes as he exhausted all the local possibilities. He always went alone. His mother had insisted on going with him once, but she was slow and held him back and the trip out was an irritation for both of them.

Joe liked his mother well enough ... well, he loved her, naturally, but at times he longed for another kind of someone. Someone a little more successful, financially that was, someone with a little money.

But his mother wasn't into all that. Not that she made a point of saying so exactly – she just wasn't. They had lived in the city up until a few years back, but when she had split with his father – who had taken off for northern India, to get in touch with his spirituality – Joe's mother had brought them both here (somewhere cheaper than London), to get in touch with hers.

Only Joe couldn't go for it really, all the hippy stuff, with the hennaed hair and the tarot cards, the evening classes in Wicca ('It's *good* witchcraft, Joe, not bad. It's the wise kind!') and all the rest.

It was all baloney. All the alternative therapies and 'getting in touch with your inner self' stuff was just a load of nonsense in his view.

Sometimes his mother would come home and say, 'I met a really spiritual guy today, Joseph. Came into the shop this afternoon. Had a real aura, you know, about him.' But he knew that all she really meant was that some guy had come into the shop and he was nice-looking and cool and she wouldn't have minded going out with him. Which was fair enough. Only why couldn't she have just said that, without making it all spiritual – without trying to make it more than it was? It really got on his nerves.

He worried sometimes that she might indeed bring somebody home who was as spiritual as she was and he would have to call him Dad or use his first name, whatever that might be. It wouldn't be anything ordinary, that was for sure. No, nobody who went into the shop ever had an ordinary name like John or Terry or Joan or Sue. Oh no, they were called Tamsin or Chare or Willow or Frond or Bagpipes or something weird like that.

He just didn't understand how she could go in for all that sort of stuff – how she could fall for it. And she knew how he felt.

'I'm afraid that one day Joseph's going to grow up and become an accountant – huh, Joe?'

It was only a joke, but it was a dig at him too, and underneath the good humour there was a real bone of contention. Joe didn't see what was wrong with money, or at least what would be wrong with having a bit more. Then they could have their own house, with space and a big garden, instead of the tiny, terraced, rented one, where the only garden was a scrap of cobbled yard and some window boxes, which were his mother's substitute for flowerbeds.

What was wrong with money? He couldn't see the harm in being able to afford to go places and not to have to worry when some furniture needed replacing. His mother and her friends seemed to look down on people who made money though. They were 'suits', 'straights' or, worse still, 'bread-heads'. Yet plenty of the hippies still played the Lottery every week. So they were plainly hoping for their million too. Sometimes they even laughed and talked about it, about what they would do when they won the Lottery jackpot. They'd open an ashram or an alternative healing centre or a commune of some kind, and they'd take care of everyone else. But Joe reckoned the real truth of it was that the winner would disappear to the Cayman Islands with his great big cheque and never be seen again, just like…

Damn it.

Everything brought it back. Every train of thought seemed eventually to arrive at that terminus. *Just like Jonah*. Gone, just like him.

'You'll make other friends, Joe,' his mother said. 'I know you will.'

Only he didn't. He wouldn't let himself. It would have seemed like an act of betrayal and he would have lost all self-respect. He was friendly enough to the others at school. He was still included in things and got his share of party invitations. But when his own birthday had come round, he'd refused to have any kind of a celebration.

'Don't you want some friends here, Joe?' his mother asked. 'How about some boys from your class?'

'No,' he told her. 'I don't want anyone. It's not right that we should sit here eating cake and having games – not if he can't be here too.'

His mother had gone a little quiet after that. She said she was going out, and he guessed that she had gone to see Aya, a friend of hers down at the Alternative Therapy and Holistic Healing Centre. They probably went on about how difficult boys were, when it was mothers who were the real problem. Sure enough she came back armed with insight and understanding and tried her best to talk him round, but without success.

Finally she said, 'Joseph, look, I know it's very, very upsetting … but it's over a year ago now. Nobody, believe me, is asking you … or wants you … in any way to forget him, ever. He was your friend, I know that. But we have to move on, Joe. All of us will remember him, always, but we have to get on with our lives. I don't want you to forget him, we shouldn't forget anyone who meant anything to us who has died and…'

The words were out before she realised what she had said. Joe stood in front of her, his face pale, his body shaking with anger and utter refusal to accept what she said.

'He isn't dead!' he told her, his voice rising. 'Jonah's not dead. He isn't dead. He isn't dead!'

He ran up to his room, slammed the door and locked it behind him. She knocked on the door, wishing that there had never been keys in the bedroom doors, resolving to take his away. She could hear him sobbing, his cries muffled by a pillow.

'Joe … Joe … I didn't mean it.'

'Go away! Go away!'

'Joe, please … I'm sorry.'

But he wouldn't let her in. So finally she left him to it, and sat up late into the night in the kitchen, waiting for him to come out. He came down at about two, red-eyed and dishevelled.

'I'm sorry, Mum. I'm sorry.'

She made them some tea, the ordinary stuff this time, not the herbal, and cut some slices of cake. There was just the two of them and Joe wished it were three. He imagined his father sitting there with them.

'Mum,' he said after a long silence, 'are men bad?'

She looked at him, shocked by his question – the way it had come out of the blue.

'What a question, Joseph. Whatever made you say that?'

'Are men bad, Mum? When I grow up, will I be bad?'

'No, no, of course not. Of course you're not bad. You're good, really good. You're honest and truthful and loyal…'

'Then why did they only ask the men?'

'I'm sorry?'

'When Jonah disappeared. The police went round all the houses and asked all the men to say where they'd been that day.'

'Yes?'

'They didn't ask any women, did they?'

'Well, I'm sure they did. They must have interviewed plenty of women, along with everyone else.'

He shook his head.

'No. It was only men. It was a man who took Jonah, wasn't it? Nobody says it, but that's what they all believe, isn't it?'

She could have given him the reassurance of a lie, but she felt that he would see straight through it. So she had to respect him and the way he was growing up so rapidly now. She nodded her head.

'Yes,' she said. 'That's what they believe. That it was a man who abducted him.'

'To do bad things?'

'…Yes.'

'So men are bad. And when I grow up, I'll be bad.'

'No, Joe, no.'

She told him the names of many good and brave, kind and honest men, starting with Jesus…

'But he wasn't a man, he was God!'

…and the Saints. And many others.

'There's my own grandad, Joseph, who died in the war. He gave his life for other people and for freedom, to fight evil and wickedness. He was a good man, brave. A hero in his way.'

That instance of someone related to him – though all he had ever been to Joe was a photograph – seemed to reassure him at last.

They went to bed and both slept in late the next morning. When Joe awoke, the milkman and the postman had already been; the bottles were on the step and the letters were lying uncollected in the hall. He went and woke his mother, bringing her a cup of her herbal tea.

Chapter 7

The Shop

It was called Mystic Moments. It was owned by Frea and Ran, witch and wizard respectively – or so they said, but Joe wasn't convinced.

It was easy to go around calling yourself a wizard and wearing weird-looking clothes and acting spiritual, but what did it amount to in the end – just that, acting, that was all. It wasn't as if either of them could actually *do* anything. If you had gone up to Frea and said, 'OK, so you're a witch then. Let's see you get hold of that brush and start flying,' she wouldn't have been able to do it. She didn't even have a driving licence for a car, never mind a broom.

As for turning people into frogs and frogs into people, she could hardly even cook. She'd just have laughed anyway, and said that that wasn't what true witchcraft was really all about, and stories of witches flying around on broomsticks had only ever been circulated by people in the past in order to oppress alternative viewpoints, stifle freedom of expression and impose a patriarchal order upon the independence of powerful women.

Whatever that lot meant. And Ran would nod along with it, like a hammer banging a nail in, to show that he was right-on about it and agreed with every word. Not that he could do any flying either. Not unless he got on to the Internet and booked himself a cheap ticket on easyJet.

No, it was all too vague, too wishy-washy. That was what Joe didn't like about it. It was like watery soup – there was nothing solid there to get your teeth into.

Ran was a Druid, or said he was. He had 'a really important position' in Druidic circles, so Joe's mum told him – which made Joe more cynical than ever. It was the 'really important' bit that did it. He was supposed to be impressed by this, was he? Here these people were, all against making money and the rat race, but they quite liked to be 'really important' too. So where was the difference? Getting on in the rat race or getting on up the greasy pole as a 'really important' spiritual type – wasn't it all about personal ambition and wanting to be taken seriously and getting power over others in some way?

Or maybe not. Maybe Joe was just too negative about it. I'm going to get a suit, he told himself, and be an accountant or a lawyer, and make lots of money.

He could just imagine their faces when he came back to visit the town. When the big, sleek car drew up outside Mystic Moments and who should step out but Joe Langley himself. He could just picture Frea and Ran's faces as he walked into the shop.

And if they asked him how he'd done it, he'd say by magic and witchcraft, otherwise known as doing his homework and passing exams – ha, ha.

They were OK though – at least their hearts were in the right place. They'd have helped anyone if they could and were always happy to listen to people's troubles and to hand out advice.

Ran used to listen, with his head cocked to one side, as if he were some kind of wise one, and he would nod and stroke at the new beard he had recently grown, possibly to make himself seem more wizardly and Druid-like. (Frea had said it looked good on him, though Joe thought it made him look like a goat.)

Quite what quality of advice he handed out was anyone's guess; it may have been good, it may have been bad or it may have been downright dangerous. But he certainly looked the part, that was true. He could look wise, even if he wasn't.

Sometimes people took advantage of them. They'd had staff working in the shop who weren't entirely honest. But they'd trust them – believing in the innate goodness of everyone – and leave them in charge of the place because they had some witchcraft and wizardry seminar to attend, or because Ran had to be at Stonehenge for the solstice. (Not that the police let the Druids get near the stones any more, but they could stand at a respectful distance and admire them.) When they came back, they'd find the till was short or there was stock missing.

'I dunno what could've happened, man. I really dunno,' the helper would say. 'I'm just not like into like adding up and accounts and things…'

It was hard to accuse anyone of deliberate dishonesty, and it wasn't that Frea and Ran were breadheads or anything like that, but they still had to make ends meet and pay the shop rent and do their quarterly VAT and present their annual accounts to the Inland Revenue. You couldn't wizard your way out of stuff like that. So they found that they couldn't leave the shop – at least not both of them together – as there was nobody they could really trust. Until Joe's mum had come along. She had been there about three years now, and they trusted her implicitly and were happy to leave her in sole charge of the place. The till always balanced when she was running it and there were never any items of stock mysteriously missing or broken. Not like it had been with her predecessor, known as Shark. Things always vanished when he was in charge, just like magic. It was uncanny, the way stuff had gone missing.

A lot of the stock was vaguely mystical – they sold the kind of things that all the hippy types liked to buy. Frea always looked a little Gothic. She dyed her hair raven black and used heavy black liner around her eyes. She was a bit spooky, Joe thought, for all that he didn't believe in witchcraft. If you'd been auditioning for vampires, you'd have put her on the shortlist. When the coffin lid creaked open in the crypt, hers was the kind of face, hair and outfit you'd expect to see.

They also sold some clothes in the shop, along with greetings cards saying things like 'Free Your Spirit' and 'Open Your Mind', and illustrated with white horses in swirling mist. In addition they stocked packets of big cigarette papers, a selection of small pipes, and they also sold pictures and posters, a lot of them of stars and strange landscapes on imaginary planets. They sold incense and joss sticks, soaps and sandalwood, henna hair dye and patchouli oil. Then there were the books; these were on subjects like crop circles, with titles like *Alien Nature – The Messages in the Fields* and *Crop Circles – Signs from Another Civilization*. They never sold any ordinary books, not like Agatha Christie or anything like that. There were plenty of paperbacks on astrology though, on fortune-telling, on reading tarot cards, on knowing your birth sign and on teaching yourself how to interpret the conjunctions of the stars.

Right at the back, hidden behind a bead curtain, there was a section on magic and witchcraft, with a sign on the bookcase reading 'Believers Only'. Some of these books seemed truly sinister, with illustrations of the Beast (whoever he was) inside. Joe had sneaked a look through most of the books at one time or another. Nobody told him not to. The Believers-Only sign didn't seem to apply to him, or maybe nobody had noticed what he was doing. Sometimes he even helped his mother to run the place when Frea and Ran were away.

Frea and Ran didn't have any children. Maybe they didn't want any, maybe they couldn't have any, or maybe they felt that children just weren't spiritual enough and that ordinary things like nappies, feeding bottles and pushing prams around might get in the way of the magic.

At the back, next to the Believers-Only books, was the paraphernalia which went with all the literature – the tarot cards, the Ouija boards, the crystal balls, the runes, the willow wands, the sticks you could use to form a hexagon on the floor.

Sometimes, when the shop was quiet, Joe would hide behind the bead curtain, staring into one of the expensive crystal balls perched on its stand fashioned into the shape of a rearing dragon. But even though he wished and willed for something to appear, the mists never cleared.

The most he ever saw was his own reflection. Even as he sat there, thinking to himself, or even whispering softly, 'Show me where Jonah is … show me what happened to him …' repeating it over and over, still nothing happened. The glass remained dark – as of course it would.

He knew that it was all rubbish. Yet he couldn't prevent himself asking. He didn't believe, but others did, and that made it a straw worth clutching at, just in case he was wrong and they were right. Only they weren't right. There was nothing to be seen in crystal balls except the reflections of those who gazed hopefully into them, desperate to see what no glass could reveal – the past, the future, their destinies, the faces of those loved and lost.

Nature abhors a vacuum, and something will soon whirl in to take possession of any vacant space. Another child sat next to Joe at school now. Someone else played in Jonah's position on the football team.

The blunt and brutal truth was that Jonah was forgotten. By the many, if not by the few. What made it all so much worse for those who did still remember him was the uncertainty of his fate. Had he died, it would have been different. In truth, it would have been better. He could have been laid to rest, properly mourned. There would have been a grave and a stone, there would have been tears and a ceremony, there would have been hymns sung and words said, and things would have been done in a proper way.

More than anything there would have been somewhere to visit, a place for Joe to go. He might not have taken flowers, because Jonah wasn't the flowers type and one boy bringing another flowers was a bit soppy. But he could have gone there and stood awhile and told Jonah things, like what they were doing in class now, and how people and places had changed.

But there was nowhere to visit. And anyway, Joe still knew that Jonah was alive. If he ever started to admit it could be otherwise, then that truly would be the end. Joe knew it was his belief that was keeping Jonah alive.

For someone who didn't go in for spiritual stuff, Joe had – whether he realised it or not – his own mysterious way of looking at things.

If the town was the hub, then the routes Joe cycled were the spokes of the wheel. He tried to vary his weekend bike rides as much as possible, but more and more he found himself drawn to one route in particular. It was a good three- or four-hour round trip, allowing time for a break in the middle.

He always started off from the centre of the town, by the war memorial, a stone obelisk that stood on a plinth in the now pedestrianised area just outside the backpackers' hotel. Joe liked to take his time to sort his things out, checking that his stuff was in the saddlebag – the puncture set and the spare inner tube, the pump and the tools.

When the music festival was on, the town was awash with people, its population swollen. At night you could hear the thud of the guitars and sometimes the cheer of the crowd, coming from the site. Joe had no interest in going. Nor had his mother, though she had been a few times in the past, when she was younger. Anyway, she couldn't have left the shop. It was one of their busiest and most profitable times of year, when the festival was on.

The noise of the festival bothered some people, but Joe didn't mind it. He would lie in bed, the windows open, listening to the distant throb of the bass, which always seemed to carry further than any other sound. He would listen to it pulsating through the warm summer-night air until he fell asleep.

One night – the third night of the festival this year – he realised, as his eyes were closing, that it would soon be fifteen months since Jonah had gone. Fifteen long months, four hundred and fifty days. He was at senior school now, and Jonah should have been there too. They should have both moved on together and been in the same class and sat near each other and gone on the trips to Bristol to see the Science Centre and the Imax cinema and all the other things that a small country town couldn't offer. What had Jonah been doing, thinking, hoping, fearing, for every minute of all that time?

Yes, the file remained open. Not even death would close it. For even that would require an explanation before the file could be put away.

Someone, somewhere, knows where he is.

The thought haunted him.

Someone, somewhere. Only who? Who was the person who knew where Jonah had gone, and why, and how?

Someone, somewhere, just carried on as normal, ate their breakfast, said hello to people, did their job and maybe even had a family and friends, commitments and responsibilities. And those people had absolutely no idea that this somebody, this person in front of them, held the key to Jonah's fate.

Once Joe had finished checking his bike, he would set off out of town, wending his way through the streets until he came to the Five Ways roundabout. Then he had to decide which way to take from there. More and more he took the last exit to the right – the route the fire engine had followed that fateful day. It led along by the Tor, up over the lower hills and then down to the all but deserted roads of the Levels.

The roads there were narrow, only wide enough for one car at a time, with occasional passing places. The only real danger was when you saw a huge tractor bearing down on you, driven by a farmer who looked like he had no intention of slowing down or stopping for man, boy or beast. Joe would pull in then, off the road, and wait on the verge for the vehicle to pass. Once or twice he had determined to go on riding, and had squeezed in so far to the side that he had almost fallen into one of the irrigation ditches, bike and all.

In the summer the heat of the sun baked the mud. Usually the wind barely stirred the trees. When it did decide to blow, it was like climbing up a steep one-in-four hill. He would ride on then, head down, counting the times he turned the pedals round, numbly determined to keep going.

The fire engine's route had been shown on television and published in the newspapers as part of the appeal for information. But where it had gone and where Jonah had gone were plainly two different things.

He rode along the same roads, to cross the same part of the Levels. He could imagine the fire engine, as wide as the road, hurtling along, the driver's hands white-knuckled as he gripped the wheel, afraid that he might put the fire engine into the ditch, the road was so narrow. He could picture a tractor coming the other way, the farmer seeing the engine coming and conceding for once that he would have to turn off and get out of someone's way. He could see the farmer's face in the cab as the fire engine whipped by, gone in a trice, the farmer wondering – just as Jonah had wondered – where the fire engine was headed and who needed saving.

Then there would have been silence again, just the swans on their nests and the herons with their long, skinny legs in the fields, the hawks in the sky and the owls buried in the foliage of the trees, fast asleep and waiting for night.

An owl had attacked him once. Joe had stopped to take a drink from his water bottle and then to pee against a tree. He didn't need to be secretive about it, there was nobody to see him. The country was flat and empty for miles. He had just finished when there was a whoosh and a sudden movement from deep in the foliage of the tree. He ducked in fear, a reflex action, not knowing what it was. An owl, maybe wakened by him, flapped out of the leaves. It went for him, trying to snatch him up, the way it would a vole or a mouse. Its talons grabbed the ridges of his bicycle helmet as it tried to carry him away. Then, realising the impossibility of its task, it released him and flew off across the Levels, flying low and possibly bleary-eyed to find a perch in a safer tree and hide in there till night.

He watched it go, excited, feeling honoured, wishing he could have told Jonah. But there was no Jonah to tell; there was no one to share it with, and by the time he got home and told his mother, the moment would have diminished. No description of it would ever do it justice.

There were times when Joe felt that the Levels knew where Jonah was; that this landscape of flat fields and hillocks of black peat, of drains and ditches and hedges of willow, had been a witness to the truth.

It knew, it knew. When he turned and looked back the way he had come he could see the Tor in the far distance, with the ruined tower upon it. He imagined when the land had been sea, and the Tor a solitary island. He imagined the wind rippling the water, blowing then, ten thousand years ago, as it blew now.

The funny thing was that people like Frea and Ran never came here. They never got out of the town most of the time. They tried to be mystical and spiritual, but they never bothered to experience the solitude of this vast, flat emptiness.

Somewhere, not far away now, was the answer to where Jonah was. But who or what could give it to him? Maybe he just didn't know how to listen. Maybe the answer was in the wind or the leaves or the sudden flight of an owl.

Or maybe he needed a cold shower. Maybe his trouble was too much imagination.

He put his water bottle back into its carrier on the frame of his bike. He stuck his foot back into the toe clip and pressed his strength against the pedals, riding on down the deserted road, a solitary figure in an empty landscape, following the strip of tarmac, letting it lead him where it would.

Chapter 8

The Woman

He'd seen her before but never spoken to her. It wasn't that she seemed particularly unapproachable, but she was always busy. Besides, although she wasn't quite his mother's age, and although she had a nice face and was pretty, she was still an adult, so what basis would there be for any relationship, or what reason for it?

He saw her as he rode by, from behind his sunglasses, which he wore even when the sky was clouded, to keep the dust and midges from his eyes. Sometimes he would stop to take them off in order to appreciate the greens and blues as they really were. He was going to buy some proper cycling glasses some day, with yellow lenses. Yellow lenses always made the world look brighter, even when it was overcast.

He saw her and she more than likely saw him as, hearing the bike, she glanced up momentarily from whatever she was doing. How much land she had he didn't know. A few acres at a guess. It wasn't a farm exactly, just a smallholding; 'a thatched cottage with stabling, outhouses and adjoining fields' would maybe have been how the estate agent had described it, the last time it went up for sale.

She had some horses, a few sheep, some goats and hens and a battered Land Rover, one of the old ones in military green, parked up by the cottage. Everything looked like it needed attention, and though she always seemed to be hard at work, the end result was never any permanent improvement.

It wasn't too shabby though; she kept things pretty well in order. The place just looked like it needed money spent on it, money that she plainly didn't have. Maybe buying the cottage had cleaned her out and now there was nothing left over. How long she had lived there Joe had no idea – he just knew that she didn't drive into town much, or he'd probably have seen her. He'd never noticed her in Mystic Moments either, buying an astrology chart or sack of joss sticks, which was a definite point in her favour.

The first few times, her presence had barely registered. She didn't even acknowledge him as he rode by – no smile, no wave, no 'Hi!', no 'Lovely day!'. Plainly not many people passed by here, but his rare appearances apparently held little value for her. He just put his head down and stepped up the speed a little, riding on by without a word.

Gradually, he began to look out for her. He would use her as a landmark. 'I'll ride to where the woman is, then when I get past I'll take a break.' Slowly a routine began to establish itself. He'd round the corner and, when he'd passed her place and she was out of sight, he'd stop and have something to eat and drink. Either that or he would take a short detour up into the local village, where he would lean his bike against the graveyard wall and go in for a while – not out of any sense of morbidity, simply because there was a bench in there and he could sit in the sun.

As time went by, and as more and more people seemed to forget all about Jonah, the more Joe would cling on to his belief that he was still alive. Yet it was a burden to him, and what made it more so was that everyone in the town knew that Joe had been with Jonah, that he had seen him run after the fire, that he had been the last person to speak to him before he had vanished, before the stranger had come – and surely it had been a stranger – to whisk him away. And worse than anything, they knew that he had delayed for two whole days before coming forward with that information.

It would have been nice sometimes just to be with somebody who didn't know all that, who didn't know that you were the last person to see the boy who had vanished from the face of the earth.

He took the route past the Tor and across the Levels more frequently. He always watched out for the woman, and slowly he came to look forward to seeing her. What he liked about her was that she wasn't like the others – like Frea and Ran and their friends – who floated about with their heads in the clouds.

She was the complete opposite. She was practical, she fixed stuff, she got on with it. She didn't pretend to be mystical and spiritual and wear funny clothes and henna her hair. She was in touch with things, like grooming the horses and collecting the eggs, repairing fences, clearing drainage channels, and she still looked pretty, even while she was doing it. She knew more about the realities of life and nature than any of them did back at Mystic Moments – or at least that was Joe's opinion.

He would have liked to have said hello to her, but he was too shy.

He overtook her once. He didn't know it was her at first because all he could see ahead was a horse and rider, and he gave the animal a wide berth as he cycled by, not wanting to startle it. He didn't have a bell on the bike, but he changed down and up through the gears so that the clatter of the derailleur would warn of his approach.

She heard, turned slightly, saw him coming, and reined in the horse. He overtook and called out, 'Thank you!' She didn't answer but raised her hand in a gesture of thanks, and then he was away. And that was it really. He just wished he'd said something more to her, but all he could think of was, 'Out on the horse today?' which sounded so totally stupid that he blushed even to have thought of it; to have said it would have been the pits.

He never saw anybody else with her. He wondered if she was married or had a 'partner'. Everyone had partners now. Hardly anybody he knew was married. Frea and Ran weren't, though they had been together a long time. Nor had his own parents been married. When things had started to go wrong, his mother had once remarked bitterly about his father, 'I won't even get the satisfaction of divorcing him!'

Though quite what satisfaction that would have brought her, he couldn't imagine. He hadn't wanted them to split up. Joe hadn't seen his father for years now. He got letters from him sometimes, with Indian stamps on their envelopes and written on thin tissue paper. He'd describe his life on the ashram and how they were all making the journey towards enlightenment. Enlightenment was all well and good, but he should have been at home with them, shouldn't he, fixing the taps and taking the bins out. Who was going to do all the ordinary stuff if everyone was going to go around being spiritual?

He bet that the lady with the cottage knew how to fix taps. He bet that she could fix anything.

A couple of weeks after seeing her on the horse, he came across her again. He had ridden past her land and not seen her, even though the Land Rover was there, so she was plainly about somewhere and hadn't gone too far. He felt a little disappointed and realised that he had selected this route deliberately with the sole purpose of seeing her; but why that should have been he did not know, or was unwilling to admit to himself.

He went on into the village, which was about two miles from where she lived. As usual he headed for the churchyard and left his bike against the wall without bothering to lock it up. Who was going to steal anything in a place like this? He took his water bottle and chocolate bar and headed for the bench. As he sat there, he saw a figure and realised it was her, down at the far end of the graveyard where the newer headstones were. She was walking among them, looking at the dates and names, but not exactly as if searching for anyone, more just looking for the sake of it, from idle curiosity.

She carried no flowers and she hadn't come with any gardening tools as some of the old ladies did. Joe had seen them, on hot afternoons, turning up with shears and rubber kneeling mats, trimming the grass on the graves of those they had lost.

The woman stopped by a cluster of headstones. He couldn't make out which particular stone she had stopped by, if any, as she was too far away and partially hidden by the branches of a tree. But he could see her looking down. He couldn't see her face and did not know what she was doing, if she was weeping, saying a prayer, or just quietly contemplating the mound at her feet. He was half compelled to go and see, but he dared not move from the bench. He even felt guilty now about coming into the graveyard to eat his chocolate bar. He had never felt this way before, but suddenly it seemed inappropriate, like bad manners.

After five minutes, the woman turned and walked away. She took the other path out of the churchyard and didn't see him, which was a relief. He was worried that she might have thought he had been spying on her.

He finished the chocolate and found a bin for the wrapper, then he walked down to where she had been standing. A number of modern headstones were there, tightly packed together, as though in the old days there had been plenty of room for people to stretch out, but now space in the churchyard was at a premium and people had to be crammed in.

He stood looking at the inscriptions and wondering which of the headstones belonged to her – if belonged was the right word. Then he gave up and walked back through the cemetery to where he had left his bike. He rode on. His route was circular, so he didn't return past her cottage, though today he was tempted to do so, just in the hope of seeing her again. Only what could he have said: 'I saw you in the cemetery'?

He resolved not to do that ride again for a while. He didn't want to see her any more, he decided. Or rather he did, but felt that he shouldn't. He felt that it was wrong of him to want to see her. Yet he couldn't have said why. He just knew that his mother wouldn't have approved of it. She kept telling him that he ought to try to be more outgoing, to release the past and move on to make new friends. But she meant with people his own age. That was obvious.

So he didn't go that way again during the winter months. He didn't do much riding anyway, for the weather had turned and even when it wasn't raining it was cold and icy and the Levels were like a skidpan. Christmas came and went and finally the daffodils appeared. It was time to put the clocks forward before he saw her again and finally spoke to her.

But before that, something else happened.

A message came.

Chapter 9

Seance

For all his self-imposed detachment and isolation, Joe wasn't completely friendless; even *he* found himself, now and again, laughing outright and enjoying the present moment so entirely that he forgot all about everything – Jonah, the past, all of it. It was like the sun coming out after days of cloud. But the shadows always returned.

With his mother's encouragement – or rather at her insistence – he finally joined in with things again, at least to a degree, and made some effort to be one of the crowd.

The problem was that anyone else was only ever a substitute for Jonah – a stopgap, pending his return, when they would have to be dropped and Jonah reinstated to his position as number-one friend. Loyalty and decency demanded no less. So part of Joe always held back – he never wholly confided in anyone or told the entire truth about his feelings. There was always a distance between him and others – his mother included. Not even she, he felt, would ever fully understand. If he tried to explain, she would misunderstand him, and somehow her misunderstanding would undermine and belittle the value of what he felt.

Most of his new friendships felt like temporary ones, which was how he liked it. If there was no prospect of them lasting – like those summer holiday friendships where you both go your different ways at the end of it – he liked it better. One of these short-lived friendships lasted for the weeks of the Christmas holiday.

The boy in question was David, Frea's nephew. It seemed odd to Joe that a witch should have something as ordinary as a nephew, but she did, and he was sent to stay with Frea and Ran over the holiday, while his mother went abroad. (To India, no doubt, Joe thought, to sort her head out, if she was at all like her sister.)

David was anything but the spiritual type. He was round and pudgy and his main interest in life seemed to be meals and the snacks in between them. He had a mournful face and a lugubrious manner, but he was good company and although he wasn't exactly active he had a dry and entertaining sense of humour.

He spent most of his time in the back of the shop reading, sitting on a three-legged stool, hidden behind the rows of trousers, coats, and silk brocade jackets. Whenever Joe came to the shop with his mother, he would join David in the back and listen to his entertaining commentaries on the people who came in to browse and to buy. He was invariably sarcastic and seemed to believe, as Joe did, that all this mystical stuff was nothing but hokum.

Then he found the Ouija boards.

There was a selection of them, in small, medium and large. This in itself struck Joe as bizarre. Small, medium and large Ouija boards. What for?

'See this?' David said to him one afternoon, showing him one of them. 'This Ouija thing?'

'What about it?'

'Know what it's for?'

'Not exactly. Fortune-telling or something, isn't it?'

'It's for getting in touch with the dead.'

Joe looked at him, wondering if this was another of his jokes.

'Really?'

'It's what it says on the box.'

'So how's that supposed to happen?'

David opened the box and took out what was inside. It was a piece of flat, folded card, about the size of a Monopoly board. He opened it up and rested it on his knees.

'All the letters of the alphabet, see?'

The letters were printed in two curved rows. The upper row ran from A to M, the one under it from N to Z. Beneath that again, printed in a straight line, were the numbers one to nine, with a zero after the nine. In the top left-hand corner of the board was a drawing of a smiling sun, and next to it the word 'Yes'. In the top right-hand corner was a crescent moon, gazing towards the sun in the opposite corner, and next to that the word 'No'. At the bottom of the board, under the numbers, was the word 'Goodbye'.

David shook the box. Something fell out. It looked a little like a thin, flattened computer mouse. He picked it up and read out the instructions on the side of the box.

'Place the planchette on the board.'

'What's the planchette? The pointer thing?'

'I suppose so.'

Joe pulled a stool up and sat opposite David. They balanced the board between them on their knees. David placed the pointer on the board, near the bottom.

'So what do you have to do?'

David squinted at the instructions on the box.

'Ask them a question and then they spell out the answer.'

'Who do?'

'The spirits.'

'What spirits?'

David answered, his voice heavy with sarcasm.

'There's bound to be spirits,' he said, 'in a place like this. In fact, I'm surprised they don't sell them.'

Joe took the box lid from him and read the instructions for himself.

'*The appropriate atmosphere is of paramount importance*,' he read. He showed the instruction to David. 'Maybe it's a misprint,' Joe continued. 'Perhaps what they meant was *paranormal* importance.'

David nodded. 'It's a load of rubbish,' he said.

'So how does it work – the spelling-out bit?'

'You both put a finger on top of the pointer, the planchette, and the spirit is supposed to guide your hands towards the right letter. But what happens, of course, is people – or one of the people – make the pointer move themselves. They might not even mean to, but they do. Because they want to believe in it, see. They want it to move. So they make it. They'd be disappointed otherwise. They want to believe there's spirits around and they're talking to them, so they make the pointer move over the board and then claim the spirits did it. It's – what do you call it? – self-delusion.'

'Yeah.'

'It's easy to prove it, because, if you close your eyes so you can't see where the pointer's going to and subconsciously guide it, all it spells out is rubbish.'

'Shall we try it then?'

'What – eyes closed?'

'Either way. I mean, I'm not going to deliberately make the pointer move.'

'Me neither. OK, put your finger on top of it.'

Joe did so. David did the same.

'*Ouija*,' David said, 'means the *Yes Yes* board. *Oui* is yes in French.'

'I know.'

'And *Ja* is yes in German.'

'I know that too.'

'All right, come on, let's concentrate.'

Even though they were at the back of a small, cramped shop, nearly every inch of which was covered with objects for sale, there was still a quiet, almost oppressive atmosphere. They were shielded from the bustle by the racks of clothes. It was like being in a small, private place, behind a heavy curtain. The ceiling of the shop had been painted black and, on top of the black, Ran had put stars and rainbows. The effect was strangely atmospheric. In a way David had been right – if there was a spirit world and if spirits were going to be anywhere, they would be here. Why not? It would almost be like a doorway for them – a portal back to the place they had left.

Their fingers rested on top of the planchette.

'No deliberately pushing it now.'

'I'm not going to,' Joe said. David was a bit too fond of telling other people what to do. 'You neither.'

'Now then ... what do we ask?'

'Ask if anyone's there.'

'OK. OK.' David swallowed and put on a solemn voice. 'Is there anybody there...?' he said softly. 'From the world of spirit?'

They both giggled. It was hard not to. Then they fell silent, and waited.

The bell above the door of the shop rang as someone came in, then rang again as someone else left. Joe could hear his mother's voice as she served a customer. It was almost Christmas, and Mystic Moments – just like any other enterprise – had got some special seasonal lines in and the shop was busy. Not that Ran and Frea actually celebrated Christmas as such, for they were self-confessed pagans. But Ran said that the concept of a midwinter festival was far older than Christianity and that pagans had got there first.

'Is anybody there ... from the world of spirit ... from the dead?' David whispered.

Strangely, David wasn't smiling any more, and neither was Joe. The atmosphere around them had become heavier, darker. At the front of the shop some incense was burning; the scent was pungent and mysterious.

'Is anybody there…?' David asked again.

The room seemed to darken, the atmosphere to become more oppressive. The sounds from the other part of the shop seemed distant now, as if everything out there was taking place behind a barrier of glass.

Joe shivered. It was his imagination doing this, he knew it. It was his own gullibility. Yet he felt apprehensive and suddenly cold.

David's face was very solemn. Vaguely worried even. His jaw tight and tense.

There was a rustle from somewhere, like a curtain billowing in the wind. Then Joe felt it, his finger moving, pushing the pointer along – almost being drawn by it. He wasn't moving it, not deliberately. It was the pointer moving him.

He looked at David. David was trying to look amused, but behind that was bewilderment, apprehension, even fear – or maybe he was just a good actor. At first Joe thought David might have been moving the planchette on purpose, as some kind of send-up, as a joke. But no. It was the pointer doing it, all on its own – or with a little outside help, maybe, from a presence unseen.

It went on moving to the top left-hand corner of the board. It stopped at the word 'Yes'.

There was someone there.

'What now?' Joe said.

David swallowed; he licked his lips. 'Let's ask who it is.'

'OK.'

Joe cleared his throat. He felt a bit foolish speaking to somebody he couldn't see. Well, all right, you did it on the telephone, but at least you knew that somebody *was* there, on the other end of the line.

'Who is it?' he said. 'Please,' he added, without really thinking what he was saying. Maybe even the spirits of the dead were entitled to a little formality and manners.

Another pause. The temperature seemed to fall. Someone must have gone out of the shop, for a draught of cold air came in from the winter street. Yet oddly the bell hadn't rung. The bell always rang when the door was opened. Or maybe it had broken again. Or maybe...

'Look!'

The pointer had begun to move.

J.

Their fingers moved with it, touching it lightly.

The pointer moved down to the next row of letters. Down and to the left. It slid along rapidly and came to a halt.

O.

Joe felt his skin tingle. His scalp seemed to be covered in an army of ants. Goosebumps rose on his arms.

'We shouldn't have started this, David. We shouldn't have started it.'

David shot a glance at him. But of course, David didn't know. He had maybe heard of the boy who had disappeared, but he probably didn't know his name.

J-O-

The pointer seemed to pause, as if whoever, or whatever, was guiding it had momentarily run out of strength. Just to spell out those two letters had taken enormous reserves of determination and its reservoir of energy was almost drained away.

Then it started to move again, to the third letter. Joe watched it, feeling so sick he wanted to run away, to get out of there. Yet he had asked the question. He had to stay for the answer. More than that, he wanted to know it, because it contradicted everything he knew. Jonah wasn't dead, he knew that. So how could the board spell out his name? How could it tell him he was...

'It's moving...'

David's voice was less than a whisper. Despite his cynicism and mockery, he watched spellbound too as the pointer moved across the board.

Only it didn't move left to find the N.

It moved across to the S. It went up to the H after that, and then rapidly down to the U and up and left to the A.

Then it stopped.

J-O-S-H-U-A.

'Joshua,' David said. 'That's an old name, isn't it? Goes back centuries. Maybe it's someone from round here.'

There were lots of Joshuas in the graveyards. Joe had seen their names on the stones.

'Ask him when he lived.'

David asked him – though surely if he had ears, even spiritual ones, he'd have heard the question already.

'When did you live?'

The pointer started to move. To the 1, to the 7, to the 9, to the...

'What the heck is going on here?'

It was Frea. She had come into the back to get a dress for a customer to try on. She walked in through the racks of clothes like someone parting heavy drapes. She looked angry.

'David – what are you doing?'

'Nothing. Just looking at this.'

She picked up the pointer, took the board from them and snapped it shut.

'Who said you could use this?'

'Well, nobody. But nobody said we couldn't either.'

Joe's mother came to see what the commotion was about.

'What's going on?'

'They were using this.' Frea showed her the board.

'Joseph...' said his mother.

'What? It was only a bit of fun.'

'And what did you do? What happened?'

Joe looked at David.

'Nothing,' he said. 'Nothing happened.'

David backed him up.

'That's right,' he said. 'Nothing. No messages,' he added.

Frea checked the board to ensure it wasn't damaged and could still be sold.

'Well, you shouldn't mess around with it. It's very serious you know, David. This isn't a toy. You can easily get in way over your head.'

'Sorry.'

'And you too, Joseph,' his mum said, not wishing to be left behind in the ticking-off stakes.

'Sorry.'

Frea was too polite to tell him off herself. She left that to his mother. She'd just deal with her nephew.

'You really shouldn't touch this,' she said, putting the Ouija board back amongst the display of crystal balls and tarot cards. 'There are many powerful things in the world of spirit, forces you simply mustn't play with, which you'll find you cannot control.'

David was behind her now, making faces. Joe saw him, but he didn't laugh. Frea took it all so seriously, she really did, but maybe this time she was right.

'It's not for children, you understand?'

'Yes, OK. Sorry,' Joe said again. 'We didn't mean anything. We were just messing around.'

Frea turned back and handed a dress in violent purple to the customer she was serving.

'It was a size ten you wanted?'

Joe thought the dress was hideous. You wouldn't even want to be seen dead in a thing like that.

In retrospect, it all seemed unreal, as if it had never happened. Yet it had. But now Joe could see how much self-delusion was involved, how either he or David must have pushed the pointer around the board, not really meaning to, but almost enjoying scaring themselves. And David was a bit of a joker too of course; he might have faked and engineered the whole thing, for his own entertainment.

Getting in touch with the dead. It was ludicrous when you thought about it – as stupid as trying to see the future inside a crystal ball. Like all that mystical hocus-pocus stuff, it was belief in the unprovable. Things like that were just confidence tricks that you played on yourself.

All the same, the Ouija board made Joe wonder; it stayed with him long after it should have been forgotten. He didn't really believe that they had got in touch with the spirit of some deceased soul, that they had spoken to two-hundred-year-old Joshua, who had maybe once been a farm worker somewhere on the Levels. But just suppose there *was* something in it, that it *was* true, that you *could* get in touch with the unseen dead in some limited way, if only to have a Yes and No conversation...

If it was possible to contact the lost and dead, then was it possible to contact the lost and living?

The thought stayed with him as he fell into sleep. In the morning it had gone, though it would often return. Right now, there was Christmas to think of – cards to send and presents to wrap; nut roast and crackers and a James Bond film on TV, which even the pagans would probably be watching.

Chapter 10

The Lamb

When the spring rain eased off, he began cycling once more. It was hard going the first few times, but he knew he'd soon get fit again.

For some reason he avoided the route that took him out by the Tor and along past the cottage. Maybe it was only to defer the pleasure of seeing the place again. Or maybe he was worried that she wouldn't be there and for some unaccountable reason he would be disappointed.

But finally his pedalling feet just took him that way. He rode along past the empty fields and past trees just starting to burst into bud after the starkness of winter. There were birds rummaging for twigs and the swans were starting to build nests on the banks of the irrigation channels – great complicated constructions that you probably needed a degree in architecture to understand. The herons stood around, alone as ever; they never seemed to be in twos. They strutted about, somehow dignified but still comical – sad but elegant clowns.

The cottage looked the same as before, its white plaster weathered and worn, the thatch of the roof mostly dark brown, except where it had been repaired. The fresh thatch was yellow, but time would turn it the same shade as the rest.

There was nobody around. A cat was hunting in the long grass, the hens were pecking in the yard and some geese were waddling about, but otherwise the place seemed deserted, the outbuildings closed.

Then he heard the lamb. He couldn't see it, but he heard its cry. It was bleating pathetically, as if in distress. He braked, stopped and looked around, but still he couldn't see where its cries were coming from. Perhaps it had fallen into one of the ditches, or was trapped in thorns, or tangled up in barbed wire.

There were always dead things on the road. Rabbits and pheasants, voles and hares, badgers and foxes. Cars and tractors ran them down, probably without even knowing. Or they killed each other. Joe had found a mole once, just lying there, looking peaceful. He had been surprised at how small it was. He had always thought of moles as being the size of hedgehogs, but this one was tiny. Or maybe it wasn't fully grown.

'Meeehhhhh!'

The bleating voice called out again, but still he couldn't see where it was coming from. It sounded more and more distressed, panicked even. He'd heard of sheep dying from fright and fear. They didn't look it, but they were highly strung. Either that or stupid. Or maybe both. Why would one rule out the other?

'Meeehhhhh! Meeehhhhh! Meeehhhhh!'

The bleating seemed to be coming from over by the gate to his left, at the entrance to the farm.

'Meeehhhhh!'

He got off his bike and wheeled it over. Then he saw the lamb. At least he saw its head. That was all there seemed to be of it, a disembodied head, opening its mouth and baaing, over and over again.

Where was the rest of it? What was it doing?

He left his bike on the ground and walked towards it. As he got near, he began to laugh. It wasn't funny really, the poor animal being in such distress, but he couldn't help it. The poor, small, skinny thing had fallen through the cattle grid.

The grid was at the entrance to the yard – there to stop animals wandering on to the road when the main gate was open. The lamb had plainly escaped from the field behind the barn, gone exploring towards the road, and then fallen down between the bars and got trapped under them. It was just tall enough to poke its head out, but that was all it could do. There was no way it could get out on its own.

Joe knelt to try and comfort it.

'You stupid thing. What did you want to go and do that for?'

The animal went on bleating. Joe reached out to stroke its small woolly head, but it only got panicky. It ducked down under the grid, scurried a short distance away, then resurfaced.

'Meeehhhhh!' it bleated again, longer and louder.

'Come on then. Let's get you out.'

He reached down again and this time it allowed him to stroke it. The wool felt soft and warm. The lamb was probably no more than a few days old. Its legs were thin and spindly. Joe wondered where its mother was, then he spotted a ewe in a nearby field, looking distressed and also bleating. That was probably her.

'Come on then, let's get you.'

It wasn't so easy though. The lamb was afraid and didn't want to come. Joe reached down and got his hands around its sides, but it struggled and made it impossible for him to pull it out.

'Come on … I'm only trying to help.'

He released it and tried again. He got the lamb by the front legs and prised it gently over the grid.

'There, that's half of you.'

Now for the rest. He reached in to lift its back legs out. It was plainly terrified.

'Don't pee on me, will you?'

The lamb started to struggle.

'Don't! Don't! You'll fall back in!'

He picked it up with both arms. The lamb became still, happy now to be rescued and carried.

Joe entered the yard and headed for the cottage. The geese looked at him with curiosity, as if wondering if he was worth the trouble of pecking, but deciding he wasn't.

'Hello!' he called. 'Anyone around? Hello! Hello!'

He saw that a door to one of the barns was slightly ajar and he headed for that, still calling as he went, not wanting to surprise anyone or for them to think that he was an intruder.

'Hello! I've found one of your lambs!'

He crossed the yard, carrying the lamb the way he had seen a lamb carried in a picture once, only he couldn't immediately remember when or where – maybe it was an illustration in a children's Bible.

He pushed the barn door further open with his foot, and entered the gloom. He hesitated by the entrance to let his eyes get used to the light.

They were walking along by the crossing when the fire engine went past and Jonah said, 'Come on! Let's follow it! Let's find the fire!' And he pelted off down the road. Joe Langley ran after him, shouting, 'No, no, we'll be late for school! Come back!'

But Jonah didn't, so Joe had to run after him as Jonah chased after the fire engine and the fire engine disappeared over the hill.

'We'll never catch it!' Joe shouted.

'It might stop at the traffic lights!'

'Fire engines don't stop for traffic lights. The only thing they stop for is fires!'

It was a ludicrous idea, and Joe knew it was, even if Jonah didn't. Jonah saw something, he wanted it, and after it he went. The impossibility of achieving his ambitions never entered his head. He always wanted what couldn't be had, yet even when he didn't get it he didn't seem disappointed. He just focused his mind on something else equally unattainable and pursued that instead.

Jonah ran on. He soon knew that Joe had given up and was no longer following him, but he didn't blame him and he didn't mind. He knew that Joe didn't like getting into trouble (not that Jonah was actually planning on getting into any, he was going to fib his way right out of it) and that was fair enough. Your friends didn't have to be the same as you and do everything you did. The difference was the point, wasn't it? You needed some things in common or it wouldn't even be a friendship, but you needed to be different too.

So he kept going. He could have done with dumping the backpack really. It wasn't easy running with that on and it was irritating having it bump against him all the time, slowing him down.

Still. Couldn't chuck it really. Might never find it again. His gran would be mad if he told her he'd lost his backpack. She didn't have much money and it wouldn't be fair. Best to hang on to it.

The fire engine was soon gone from sight but the siren remained clearly audible, so he ran after that. There were only so many roads out of town after all, and he had a pretty good chance of picking the right one. Anyway, maybe he'd see the smoke soon, or he could ask somebody.

'Fire engine go this way, mate?'

They only had to say yes or no. He didn't have to explain anything, or why he wanted to know. For all they knew it might be his house that was burning.

So he kept going. Even if he never found the fire, it was a day out. Nice weather, nice change. He'd find something to do. Or if he did get bored after an hour or two, he could go into school for the afternoon – or whenever he felt like it, come to that – and say he'd been at the dentist or his gran had been ill or something. There was always a way around it with a little cheek and imagination.

He took a short cut down an alley. It was funny really, he'd lived in this town all his life and yet he'd never been down this alleyway before. Just never had a reason. He darted down it. It was dank and narrow. If you reached your arms out, you could touch either wall as you ran along. The ground was cobbled with ancient stones.

They weren't like the newcomers, him and his gran. They hadn't moved from the crowded cities for a better, cleaner, quieter, less stressed and pressured way of life. They hadn't been attracted by legends or ley lines or corn circles or auras of mysticism and spirituality. It just happened to be the place they had been born in, no better and no worse than a hundred other country towns. The Tor was just a landmark to them, a hill, that was all. They didn't believe it meant anything, that there were spiritual forces attached to it.

You didn't have time for stuff like that when you had to get the cows in – which had been what most of his family had done, until mechanisation had meant fewer and fewer jobs in farming and they had moved into town.

He came to the end of the alleyway and, without hesitation, took the turning to the left. It had to be a short cut to the Five Ways roundabout and the open road, and then he'd be right for the fire engine. Perhaps he should head up the Tor. From there he might be able to see the fire engine again, as it drove over the Levels. He'd have a view of several counties from way up there. You'd see smoke from miles away.

'Hey!'

'Sorry!'

He'd almost run into the door of a car.

'Careful!'

'Sorry!'

He helped pick up the things from the street, the packages and carrier bags. He did it quickly, impatient not to lose time and miss the fire engine.

'There. Sorry.'

'Calm down, son. Where's the fire?'

He grinned widely.

'Dunno, but I'm following it.'

'You're what?'

He grinned again, pleased with himself – with the sheer cheek of it.

'I'm following the fire engine.'

A laugh, a look of amusement.

'You'll need to run fast to catch that!'

'I'm going to try. Think it's heading for the Levels.'

He sprinted on a few yards then heard a shout from behind him.

'Hey, son! I'm going that way myself. Do you want a lift?'

He hesitated. A lift. He'd get there then, no trouble. And the man looked all right – decent enough.

He almost said yes. Then he remembered his gran, the teachers, the policeman and the policewoman who had come to the school.

What must you never do?

Go with a stranger. Even when they seemed nice and friendly and kind. Never accept a lift, not from anyone.

He shook his head and said, 'No thank you. I'm fine, thanks.'

Then he turned and he was running again, faster than ever, in pursuit of the fire engine and the fire.

He had remembered his gran's words about strangers, and he had done the right thing. She'd have been pleased with him. She'd have been proud.

Joe realised that he was still wearing his sunglasses and that was why everything inside the barn looked so dark. He managed to reach up and take the glasses off without letting the lamb go. It wasn't struggling now and seemed quite docile, but it was heavier than it had looked.

'Hello! Hello?'

There was a figure at the far end of the barn, crouched down over something lying in the straw. There was a glint of silver in the dim light. The figure held a knife and was, Joe could now see, kneeling over another shape, which appeared to be moving, struggling even.

'Hello! I found one of your lambs. It was stuck under the cattle grid. It must have fallen down.'

The door swung shut behind him. The barn smelt of animals and straw. Dust floated in the air. He squatted and placed the lamb down on the floor. It stood there, staying by him. He had half expected it to run away.

'I thought I ought to get it out. It doesn't seem injured. Just thought I'd come and tell you, that was all.'

The rest of the world seemed far away, the way it does sometimes when a door closes, shutting everything out, making it no longer matter, making what is inside seem to be the only real and important thing.

The kneeling figure looked up at him. If she was grateful, she didn't say so.

'There's some twine over there,' she said. 'A ball of it. On a nail. Bring it over, would you?'

He looked around, saw a ball of waxed string dangling from a nail amongst some tools. He presumed it was what she meant and went to get it.

'There's a small pair of cutters next to it. Bring them too.'

He took them down and brought them over. He realised, as he drew nearer, that the animal smell was more pungent, and that there were smears of blood on her clothes and on the straw. Something seemed to be struggling, close to where she knelt.

'OK. Come and help me. Just help her push. Press down there.'

Half repelled and half fascinated, Joe knelt down beside the woman. A ewe was lying on the straw, in the throes of giving birth. It started to bleat, loudly and plaintively.

'OK, come on now.' She tried to help speed the delivery. Then she looked concerned. 'Damn! It's twisted!'

The woman reached inside and moved the lamb, helping the ewe to give birth. Not really knowing how he was supposed to help, Joe just knelt there, pressing – probably ineffectively – against the sheep's side, making encouraging noises and saying things like, 'There, there,' and, 'It'll be OK,' though he had no idea if it would be.

The head of the lamb appeared. Joe watched, amazed and horrified. The lamb's eyes were closed and its fleece was wet with some oily-looking stuff.

Then suddenly the ewe half reared, almost as if trying to stand. She arched her back, strained and then sank on to the straw. Joe looked down – almost as if he shouldn't be looking, as if at any moment somebody was going to tell him that a boy of his age had no business…

'Look… '

The woman was smiling. The lamb was born. There it was, its eyes open, its small body seeming to unfold like the petals of a flower in the sun.

'Pass that, would you?'

He handed her an old towel, which lay on the straw.

'And some clean water? Tap's there.'

He picked up a plastic bucket, took it over to the tap, tipped its murky contents down into the small drainage channel and filled it up with fresh water. He glanced over to see what she was doing – something with the knife and the cutter. He turned away and watched the bucket fill. He looked back. She had put the knife away now, that bit was over. He felt a little better.

He turned off the tap and carried the bucket across.

For the first time she looked at him properly.

'Thanks.'

She soaked the towel and rinsed it out, then used it to clean the mucus from the lamb. Its mother lay panting on the straw.

'You want to hold him?'

Joe nodded. The one he had found outside had looked small, but this one was tiny by comparison. She picked it up and passed it over to him. He took it in his arms. It was already so perfectly formed; that was the amazing thing. It had the lot – legs, eyes, ears, fleece. It was small and slender too, quite unlike the fat blob-shaped bundle of wool with sticky-out legs that it would grow into. It was the other way round for people – they started off fat and got leaner; sheep started off lean and got fatter. It was a shame it had to grow up, to turn from something so waif-like and elegant into just another ordinary thing.

He stroked the lamb's back. Its fleece was smooth and soft, damp and warm. The animal looked at him and started to bleat, its eyes huge and appealing.

'He wants his mother – and I think she wants him too.'

Joe set the lamb down carefully. It wasn't used to having legs yet and stood on them as if they might suddenly collapse. Then it made its unsteady way over to its mother, tottering with awkward but somehow elegant movements – full of the charm of the newly born.

It was born to die, Joe thought. Well, everybody was, eventually, but that wasn't what he meant. He meant that it would die too soon and probably not from natural causes. It was economics, that was all. It might not even get past being a lamb. It might never grow up at all. A few months, maybe, and that would be it. Like a lamb to the slaughter – wasn't that the expression? The young, the helpless, the innocent...

For a second he thought of Jonah again, but then he squeezed the thought from his mind. Why let it spoil the here and now? The lamb would be outside soon, gambolling in the field, running about with the others, pleased to be alive.

The woman was washing her hands. She dried them on another towel, then she smiled at him.

'Thanks.'

'That's OK.'

She extended her hand.

'I'm Anna.'

Joe was pleased that she had a proper name, an ordinary one – that she didn't call herself Fez or Grizelda or Lucinda of the Levels.

'Joe,' he said.

'Would you like a drink? I'm going to make some tea. Or there's milk or juice.'

'Well...'

'Or some Coke in the fridge.'

'Well, I wouldn't mind a Coke. Thanks.'

He followed her to the door of the barn. When she pushed it open the sky looked startlingly bright.

'How about the lambs?'

'They'll be OK now. Just leave the door open. I'll see to them in a while.'

They crossed the yard to the cottage. Hens, geese and ducks scuttled away.

'You ever seen a lamb born before?'

'No,' Joe admitted reluctantly, feeling that he should have done somehow.

'Ever seen anything born before?'

'I saw an egg hatch out once,' he said. 'In a film.'

'Well, that was something.'

She pushed the kitchen door open and Joe followed her inside. He realised that his heart was beating fast and that his skin was flushed. He was just excited – excited and proud to have seen the lamb born, to have helped it arrive; to have been instrumental in its existence.

Nobody he knew had ever done a thing like that – no one in his class, no one at home or in the shop. Not his mother or Frea or Ran. Ran thought he was a wizard and said he was a Druid and all the rest, and at one with all the powers of the universe, but he had never seen a lamb born, Joe would bet on that. So what did he know then? He didn't know anything.

Joe felt proud and far more grown up than he had felt twenty minutes ago, when he had been riding his bike along the road, past the cottage gate. To have seen something born, it was half of life.

Only what did that make the other half?

'How about some cake?' Anna asked, handing him a can of Coke.

A fruitcake lay cooling on the sill, covered in a muslin cloth to protect it from insects.

'Well…'

'I'm having some myself. I'm cutting it anyway.'

'Oh, OK. Thanks.'

She sliced the cake and made conversation as the kettle boiled. She did most of the talking and he just answered with 'Yeses' or 'Noes'. He still felt shy with her.

He watched her as she talked. Pretty but practical, he would have said. His mother and Frea were pretty too, but not so practical. If they'd come across a sheep about to give birth, they'd probably have panicked and rung for an ambulance.

He guessed that maybe she was his mother's age after all. He had thought that she had looked younger, but maybe that was the tan. Being outdoors a lot had darkened her skin, but it hadn't given her wrinkles, at least not yet.

'There you go. Here – sit down.'

He accepted the slice of cake and the proffered chair. They sat at the table together.

'It was lucky you came along,' she said.

But he knew that even if he hadn't happened along she would still have managed without him.

'Oh, I didn't do much,' he said.

She broke a piece of cake off and put it into her mouth; she had white, almost perfect teeth.

'Have I seen you before sometimes?' she asked.

'Maybe,' he nodded. 'This is one of my routes.'

'Bike routes?'

'That's right.'

'You go on your own?'

He felt embarrassed for some reason.

'Yes. Well, I do mostly. I do now.'

'You don't have a friend to go with?'

'No, I did … but I just go on my own now. I don't mind. I quite like it. Sometimes I like to be alone.'

'Me too,' she said. Then she smiled. 'It's less trouble that way.'

He looked at her shyly, feeling he knew what she meant, but not knowing how to respond. So he just kept silent and ate the cake.

'Another slice?'

'No, I'm OK.'

'Sure? There's plenty.'

'No, I'm OK, thanks.'

She got up and took the plates over to the sink. Maybe that was a hint that she was busy. Whether it was or not, he took it as such.

'Well, I'd better be going. Thanks for the cake.'

'You're very welcome, Joe. And thank you for rescuing my lamb.'

'Oh, that's all right.'

She stood up.

'I'll walk out with you.'

They left the kitchen and strolled across the yard. The lamb he had pulled from the cattle grid was skipping around, its ordeal forgotten.

'It's the one returned to the fold, huh?'

He didn't understand her.

'I'm sorry?'

'Don't you know that story? About the lost lamb? How there's always celebration over the lamb returned to the fold, or when the wanderer comes home. The good shepherd just never gives up looking – that's the moral, I guess.'

He thought of Jonah again. He thought he'd squeezed the thought out for a while, but it was back.

'Yes. Yes.'

'Well, thanks again. I'd better go and see how mother and child are getting on. Bye then.'

'Bye.'

He walked towards the gate and to where he had left his bike. On an impulse he turned and called back to her, just as she was entering the barn.

'Anna!'

'Yes?'

'Can I come back some time and see how the lambs are doing?'

'Sure. Any time you like.'

She waved to him and disappeared into the barn.

He got back on to his bike and rode on.

Although, strictly speaking, he'd already had a break, he stopped again when he arrived at the nearby village.

Despite the fruitcake he'd just eaten, he made his way to the bench in the churchyard and sat down to have his chocolate bar.

He thought of the lambs, the two of them, the one he had rescued and the one just born. He glanced at the church windows, searching until he found it, and there it was, picked out in stained glass – the almost universal Christian image of Jesus carrying a lost lamb, returning it to the fold.

He walked among the gravestones again. This time he read the names and dates more closely. As the years passed, the first names changed with the fashions of the times. They started off as Ebenezer, became Wilf and Cuthbert, then changed to Anthony and Philip. The women's names went from Mercy to Gladys and Winifred, then to Tara and Jane. He didn't know anybody called Winifred or Gladys. Not in his class.

Then he came across a small headstone under the branches of an expansive willow. It was smaller than all the others in the yard, as if to indicate that the body it marked was also little, that it was different, special, and to be distinguished from the almost exclusively adult company around it.

Joe had overlooked the stone before, it was so small and well hidden, sandwiched amongst other, larger stones, and concealed within the shadows. He paused to read the name and the other words on it. It said that the remains of Matthew Starne lay here, and then gave his dates. Joe looked at them in wonder and then read them over again, certain he had misread and made some mistake. The year of Matthew Starne's birth was the same as Joe's. They had been born at the same time of year, at the end of September.

He would have been my age, he thought. At my school maybe. In my class. There weren't many secondary schools in the district – primary, yes, but, when they got older, children were bused from the villages to the nearest town. The council said it couldn't afford to maintain secondary schools in outlying rural districts.

My age, my class. Just like me. My enemy or my friend. Or just indifferent to me.

He stood looking down at the grave, thinking of the dead boy and all the things he could have been. Then he read the dates again, sure he had made some mistake. But he hadn't.

Matthew Starne had been born on the twenty-fifth of September and had died on the twenty-sixth. He had lived for only one day.

Joe remained there in the churchyard for longer than he had intended. The strands of so many events entangled themselves in his mind, and he tried to disentangle them and turn them into some kind of coherent pattern, to make sense of such disconnected things.

There was the newly born lamb, fresh into the world, skinny-legged and kicking, still damp and new, and here was a boy who had also come into the world, just as the lamb had, but who had only lived for a day, one day out of all the days he should have been entitled to.

Three score years and ten was a lifespan, or so it said in the Bible. A score being twenty. He remembered that. Old-fashioned measures of old-fashioned quantities.

Seventy years. And that was a low estimate now. People often lived far longer, at least in developed countries they did. They'd learned that in geography.

Say eighty then. He might have lived for eighty years. That was … what … thirty thousand days, something like that? And he had had one, that was all.

Even the lamb would get more, even if it only lived for a few weeks before it was taken to the slaughter.

And then there was Jonah, his days uncounted, unknown, just vanished. How did he pass his days? Where? Or was Joe wrong in his continuing belief in

Jonah's existence? Had his days long since come to an end?

If only there was some way to know. It wouldn't be so bad if only he could discover even a fragment of the truth.

Then it occurred to him that perhaps there was a way to find out, if he was willing to believe in it and to try it. Maybe he would soon. Yes, maybe he would.

He took one last look at the headstone before turning away and walking back to where he had left his bike. There were no flowers, not even a metal vase for them as there was by most other graves, set into the earth so that neither wind nor rain would knock it over. Yet the grave seemed not entirely ignored. It was reasonably tidy, though the grass needed cutting. Maybe whoever had tended it had stopped coming by. Perhaps giving it attention was more distressing than neglecting it.

He took his bike and wheeled it out of the churchyard and on to the road. He cycled home, taking his time, thinking about everything that had happened, wanting it all to make sense. There was Jonah, there was the headstone of the boy who had only lived for a day, there was the newly born lamb and there was the one he had rescued too, the one that would have been trapped forever if left to its own devices. It could never have escaped on its own; it would have starved to death.

But as he neared home he realised that all these things were just random and unconnected. All there really was was chaos. The only order that existed was the one imposed by your own mind.

He hadn't been home long when his mother returned from her job at the shop.

'I'll do tea in a minute,' she said. 'First I'm going to try and fix this tap.'

She had bought some washers from the hardware store to fix the annoyance of the dripping tap in the kitchen. She turned the water off and tried for a while to take the tap apart, but she wasn't able to do it.

'It's no good, we'll have to get a plumber after all.' She had been trying to avoid the expense. 'Or maybe we can live with it a while longer. Just imagine it's a nice sound, like a wind chime.' She thought a moment. 'Perhaps I could ask Ran to do it.'

Ran, Joe thought, couldn't fix a hole in a paper bag with a roll of Sellotape. No, he probably knew a dozen spells for fixing leaking taps, but give him a spanner and he'd just stare at it and wonder what it was. He'd probably think it was a wand.

As his mother got the food ready, and as the rice simmered in the pan to the accompaniment of the dripping tap, he thought of Anna, back on the small farm – how she had a whole collection of tools hanging from hooks on the barn wall. She could deliver lambs and probably fix machines – a dripping tap was something she'd be able to sort out in a moment.

He thought of his mother's feeble efforts and felt a certain amount of disgust. She ought to be able to change a washer on a tap, surely. Everybody ought to have at least that much self-reliance.

'Shall I fix it, Mum?' he offered, convinced that he would be able to do it, if only he was allowed to try.

But she wouldn't let him. She was worried that he might flood the kitchen. Her attitude angered him. Sometimes she treated him as if he were still a five-year-old.

'On second thoughts, I'll ring up the landlord,' she said. 'I don't see why we should have to get a plumber in to do it. It's his responsibility, after all, things like that.'

Chapter 11

The Ouija Board

Towards the second anniversary of Jonah's disappearance, an enterprising journalist, one with a good memory – or with a good filing system – was moved to remember him.

He wrote an article in one of the national newspapers asking where the boy was, what had happened to him and where the police investigation had gone wrong. He castigated the authorities for their failure to find him and to 'protect the children of this land' who were surely 'entitled to expect better' from those who 'were supposed to protect them' as were 'their loving parents' who 'paid enough in taxes' but 'got little by way of law and order in return'.

And as for the people who had been responsible for his disappearance – people lurking in the midst of decent communities, who maybe even now were preparing to strike again – they should be locked up and the key thrown away. The journalist interviewed some locals, who spoke of their real worries and concerns that such a person might still be at large.

The article covered the two middle pages of a newspaper which Joe's mother purported never to buy (it wasn't '*serious*' enough), but which she enjoyed furtively reading nonetheless, and which she sometimes brought home from the shop, claiming a customer had left it, or that it was Frea's and she had finished with it.

The journalist had also interviewed the senior detective still nominally in charge of the case. She said again that the file 'had not been closed and never would be closed' and that enquiries were 'still active' until such time as the boy (or his remains) were found.

There were two photographs of Jonah. One of him as he had been – the one cropped from the class photograph taken shortly before his disappearance – and one (according to the projections of some computer software) as he would look today: older, taller, broader, his face filled out a little, his cheekbones stronger and more defined.

Joe pored over the photographs for a long time. He got out the old class photo and looked at himself in it. Then he went to the mirror to see how he had changed between then and now, and to thereby assess how accurate, or inaccurate, the computer-generated image of Jonah might be. It was hard to tell. How did you – or any computer software – know how someone might age? Ageing was more than a genetically driven thing; surely what happened to you in life could affect your appearance as much as your genetic code.

It was a convincing picture though. It was eerie to see him – the same Jonah, the same face, just older, more mature.

Where Is He Now? the headline asked, quite unable to answer its own question, but anxious to hold to account those who should have been able to.

The article listed other failures, other people who had disappeared, never to be seen again. It listed the number of people who went missing every year; there were thousands. They all seemed to have vanished like ghosts. Many had gone out for a moment, they had popped down to the shops, they had packed no bags and carried no luggage; some had even taken no money, they had only the clothes they wore and the shoes they stood up in.

But they had vanished just the same, leaving worry and distress behind them, and anxious, grieving relatives, begging them just to get in touch. A phone call was all they wanted, no more than that. Or they wanted to say that they were sorry, that all was forgiven, or that the misunderstanding was all cleared up now and as for that matter which had caused all the trouble, it would never be mentioned again. If only ... only ... only ... the missing person would please ring home.

Shortly after the publication of the article, people began to call in with sightings of Jonah. They had seen him in the company of a well-dressed man, eating burgers in the motorway services. A couple returning from a trip to Spain thought they had spotted him in a village, high up in the mountains. They had only got a quick glimpse, and he seemed more suntanned than in the photograph, but it could have been him easily, in fact they were sure it was. But it wasn't.

The sightings continued to pour in for the next fortnight. Each one was investigated as far as it was possible to do. But they all led to nothing. Silence swirled back in again, like mist to a hollow. There were other indignant articles in newspapers, complaining of other scandals and other public failures, about the waiting lists in hospitals, about the state of pensions, about immigration. Jonah was again forgotten by the world at large. But Joe went on remembering him with ever increasing determination, holding on to his memory as if by doing so he was stopping Jonah from falling into some dark, bottomless lake of oblivion.

At first Joe thought of stealing the Ouija board, but in the end he decided against it. It wasn't a sense of honesty that stopped him, just the fear and embarrassment of getting caught, and the repercussions.

It would have been simple enough to do it though. He had every reason to be in the shop; he was often there, sitting in the back, maybe doing some homework, waiting for his mother to finish. He stayed out of the customers' way and Frea didn't seem to mind him being there, so it would have been very easy indeed. He could just have taken the box and put it into his bag and who would have been the wiser?

Only what if Frea had suddenly appeared, just as he was doing it? What if she had caught him? What would she have said? What about his mother too? Maybe Frea would have asked her to give up the job and leave. There were notices up too, saying Shoplifters Will Be Prosecuted. You didn't expect shoplifters in Mystic Moments, but you got them. Some people would steal anything – even books telling them stealing was wrong.

So he decided to make his own. He took one of the Ouija boards out of its box, just to refresh his memory as to how it was laid out, then he took the knowledge home and made his own version in the privacy of his room, fashioning it from some stiff card. He painted the letters of the alphabet in two rows, one above the other. He outlined them first, taking time and trouble to make it all look professional. Then he painted the letters in, careful not to smudge anything or to let the edges run. Then he added the numbers and the words Yes and No and Goodbye. He even painted a sun and moon.

Next he varnished the card so that the surface would be perfectly smooth and the pointer would be able to glide over it easily. He wondered about the pointer – the planchette – but decided in the end not to make one. He had read that a small, upturned glass would work equally well in spelling out any message.

Yet when it was all completed and done, he hesitated to use it. He just hid it away in the back of the cupboard, underneath the pile of board games that he no longer played with but refused to send to the charity shop. They were too full of the past, of wet days and long afternoons, of rain running down the windows, of cold outside and warmth within, of winter dark and the lights on early. He'd played those games with his father, back when they were all still together in another town; he'd played them with Jonah, who didn't have a father either by then – or not a proper one.

So he wouldn't give them away. It would have been like giving his past away – like losing part of his life, or throwing away old, precious photographs.

He left the board in there, wondering why he had made it when he was so full of doubt and cynicism. Was it really possible to converse with the dead? Because if the dead *were* really there and you *could* communicate with them, why didn't they tell you something interesting, something important, like what it was like to be dead, what to expect? Why did they only ever say things like, 'Aunty says not to worry,' and 'Steve says all is well'? Was that the best they could manage? Was that all they had to say? They had been on the strangest and most feared of all journeys, but had nothing interesting to report.

But say … just say … that there was something in it. A minuscule, infinitesimal little something. Did he have the right then not to try it, to leave this one stone unturned? It wasn't for his benefit, after all. It was for Jonah.

Anyway, it wasn't the dead he wanted to get in touch with.

It was the living. Jonah was alive. He had to be. He had no choice in the matter – Joe willed it to be so.

There was another problem. He needed someone else. He felt that it wouldn't work alone. Left to himself, he would, consciously or otherwise, influence the movement of the glass across the board. He would make it spell out what he wanted it to, which wouldn't be right. It had to come *through* him, not from him.

He needed somebody to do it with, and there was no one. He could think of absolutely nobody to ask whose involvement would not complicate everything. There was only David and he hadn't been back since Christmas. He might not come back again for some time. So who else was there? Not his mother, nobody he could think of at school, not Ran or Frea. There was nobody who wouldn't ask difficult questions, or criticise him, or tell him not to meddle – who wouldn't sit in judgement.

Or maybe there was.

There was one person he knew who might help him, who wouldn't tell him he was being presumptuous or ridiculous or was meddling where he had no business or getting in out of his depth. He felt it instinctively. Yes, there was one person who might help him.

It was only a matter of asking.

Jonah ran on. He was lost now and had, he knew, no hope of catching the fire engine or finding the fire. He slowed to a jog and then slowed even more until he was ambling along, swishing at the hedgerows with a long stick that he had found on the verge.

Then he had an idea. He stopped, threw the stick away, and looked for a fat-bladed piece of grass, which he tore off and flattened between his thumbs. He held his thumbs up next to his mouth and blew, using the grass as a reed. A high-pitched, squeaky note emerged. He laughed and did it again. The blade of grass flapped from side to side and the note got higher and lower.

He ambled on down the road, making the awful, irritating noise – only there was nobody but himself to irritate.

He'd lost the fire engine, but who cared? He looked at his watch. It was too late for school now. He may as well take off the rest of the day. He had some money, only, looking around, he saw that there was nowhere to spend it. There were flat fields all around him. Pity, he could have done with a drink. He stopped and peered at the contents of one of the irrigation channels. The water looked green and disgusting. He wasn't drinking that.

Well, no sense in turning back yet. He'd just end up back at the town and somebody might see him and ask why he wasn't at school. He might as well go on. He'd find a village eventually, and it would have a shop – one that wouldsell everything: groceries and stamps and hardware. He'd get himself a bag of crisps and a drink.

He took off his sweatshirt and stuffed it into his bag. He was hot, but that wasn't the only reason. His sweatshirt had the school crest on it and told people where he belonged. Nothing else about him said that he should have been at that school. If anyone asked he'd tell them some kind of a story, about a dental appointment, or something of that kind.

Not that anybody was going to ask. The place was deserted. Just the big, stupid birds and the sound of machinery in the far distance as the diggers munched up the peat and stacked it into heaps.

Then around the corner, in the middle of nowhere, he found something interesting – a great big yard of scrap and junk, hidden by a clump of trees. Architectural Salvage, the sign outside said. Jonah decided to go in. There were a few cars and some people mooching around. There was stuff lying everywhere, some of it out in the open, probably more of it inside, under cover, in the long sheds around the yard.

There was a tank. A real tank. He hurried over to see it. It had old Soviet military markings on the sides and Russian lettering. He climbed up on to the front of it and tried to pull the top up, hoping to get inside, but it was welded shut. Pity. He'd have liked that, to see inside a tank. Wait till he told Joe about it. He'd never believe him.

He found a rocket launcher too. What it was doing there, he had no idea. It wasn't exactly architectural, unless you were maybe thinking of putting it in the front room as some kind of conversation piece.

There were signs up saying, This Yard Is Dangerous and, Enter At Your Own Risk. But nobody seemed to notice him, not even the men who worked there. Everyone seemed to think he was with somebody else.

He wandered through the sheds. One was full of old baths, another was stacked high with toilets, a third held old church pews and a fourth old fireplaces. There was a big heap of toilet lids too, lying one on top of the other, like a pile of coins.

Eventually he got bored with it all and felt he had seen enough. He had hoped to find a Coke machine, or maybe a tap, but there wasn't anything. He would have asked one of the men who worked there, only he might have responded with awkward questions or become suspicious and wondered what Jonah was up to.

So he left and continued on his way. He still had hours to kill. He'd find a village and a shop and he'd get some crisps and a drink and maybe a chocolate bar, then he'd sprawl out in the sun on the green next to the duck pond, or behind some trees where no one could see him. He'd lie there in the warm sunlight and let his eyes grow heavy and maybe even close for a while. Then when he woke he'd go back to the shop for another drink, and then he'd turn for home.

He'd get in and his gran would say, 'That you, Jonah?' as if it could be anyone else. And he'd say, 'Only me, Gran,' and she'd say, 'Tea in an hour or so.

Got much homework? Biscuits in the tin if you want one.' And he'd say, 'I'll start it in a minute,' and he'd take a couple of biscuits and go and watch some telly for a while.

He'd not mention the fire engine or anything like that. Later in the evening he'd type a note on the old typewriter and sign it with her name. Her signature was such a scrawl nobody would even know he'd done it. Then he'd hand the note in tomorrow, apologising for his absence, saying he was a bit poorly and under the weather. If he'd missed anything important, Joe could fill him in on it. But he doubted he had. It was only one day, after all. It wasn't as if he made a habit of it. It wasn't going to matter.

So on he walked, towards the village at which he was sure he would soon arrive. But the journey lengthened and the village did not appear, and by now his thirst was raging. He was as parched and dry as a brick.

Chapter 12

The Name

Joe wanted to go back and see the lambs. He had even started to think of the one he had rescued from the cattle grid as 'his'. Then at other moments it would be the one he had seen born which belonged to him. Or maybe it was both.

But he didn't go, not immediately. The following Saturday, a week after the birth of the lamb, he took a different route, the Saturday after that another one again. On both occasions he chose the rides deliberately, not exactly to spite himself, but because he wanted to return to the farm so much that to go back too soon would betray his eagerness, which, for reasons he could not quite explain to himself, he wished to conceal. At least from her.

So he waited. He found the other bike rides tedious and dull. The sky was grey on both occasions, the Levels dull and uninteresting. It drizzled on that second Saturday. He had to stop and put on waterproofs.

On the third Saturday he went back. Three whole weeks had gone by. The lambs would be bigger, quickly growing up. He might not even recognise them if he left it any longer. So he set off in the direction of the small farm and the village beyond it.

He was hoping that she would be out in the open fields. That way it would be easier. He would see her and call hello – or, who knew, she might even see and wave to him first – and he could go on from there. She'd be sure to tell him how the lambs were and ask if he wanted to see them. It would be easier if he got an invitation, much easier than having to ask. There might even be more cake and Coke in it.

But he was out of luck. As he neared the smallholding he slowed his pace. His eyes searched the fields for her, but she wasn't to be seen. He stopped his bike, pretended that he thought he had a puncture, upturned the cycle and inspected the wheels. Maybe she was in the barn. If he lingered she might come out. He got the pump off the frame, put a little air into the tyres, put the pump back – still she did not appear.

There was silence, like a blanket of fog. He realised how remote the place was, so far from anywhere, how narrow and unfrequented the road. He turned and looked behind him. In the far distance was the Tor, way back on the horizon, barely a bump on the endlessly flat land.

He felt that someone was watching him, listening out for him – had been waiting for him, expecting him even.

A cloud crossed the sun and a great, swift, running shadow raced over the Levels, sprinting with the light behind it as if shadow and sunlight were in a race to be first to the end of the fields.

He felt the cool of the shadow, shuddered briefly with the chill, and then felt the warmth of the sun again. The leaves of the willows and the aspens quivered in the light breeze. The lambs, unnaturally silent for so long, began to bleat.

It was no good. If he wanted to see them he would have to go and knock at the cottage door.

Maybe nobody was there. Perhaps she had gone into town, or to the agricultural merchants to pick up some spares or some feed. He couldn't see the Land Rover, but it might be inside the rickety wooden garage, which looked like a collection of nailed-together planks, slowly falling apart.

In which case, if she wasn't there, he could just go and see the lambs anyway. She wasn't going to mind if she wasn't there and, anyway, she had said that he was welcome to come and see them.

'Hello! Hello!'

He wheeled his bike over the cattle grid and into the yard. Its surface was rutted with baked mud.

'Hello! Anyone in? I came to see the lambs!'

Though in truth he was disappointed at her absence. He had come to see her too.

'Hello! Hello!'

Nothing. Nobody. He left his bike against the side of the barn and walked towards the field where the lambs and ewes stood grazing. The lambs were still pleased enough with life to run about for the sheer joy of it. The sheep seemed dull and staid by comparison, sensible and middle-aged and only interested in their food.

He went to the gate and stood on a lower rung, looking into the field for his lambs, especially for the one he had rescued, wondering if it might remember him and come over and lick his hand. It had distinctive markings: a mottled coat and a black face.

But no, if it remembered him it didn't notice him now, or it wasn't grateful enough to come and show its appreciation.

He climbed up on to the next rung, thinking that he might hop over into the field and go across to stroke its fleece, when...

'Hello?'

She frightened the wits out of him. He hadn't heard a sound. She was just suddenly there, right behind him, as if she had come from nowhere, or had popped up from a hole in the earth.

'Oh, hi, hello. I'm sorry, it's me, who found the lamb, remember, under the cattle grid, and you said it was all right for me to come back and see them again and anyway I did shout and I knocked on the door but there was nobody there so I just thought I'd look at them and then I was going to go...'

She smiled, amused by his consternation.

'No, that's OK. I didn't recognise you at first. Carry on.'

'Can I go into the field?'

'Yes, but be careful. Don't startle the ewes. They're protective. They'll go for you if they think you mean any harm.'

'No, I'll just look.'

'Come over to the cottage when you're done.'

'Um ... OK ... if that's all right.'

'Sure. I've a few things to do first. I'll be ten minutes.'

She walked off across the yard and left him to it. He still couldn't work out how she had appeared so suddenly. It was almost as if she had come from nowhere, like a ghost.

But the sound of her wellingtons on the baked mud was real enough, and the noise of the barn door. The bleating of the lambs was real enough too, and the birdsong and the whistling wings of a swan overhead as it struggled to carry its weight through the air. Then he thought he heard another sound, the sound of his own name being called. He turned to see who wanted him. But it was just the breeze sighing in the willows and blowing softly through the grass.

He climbed over into the field and went to look at the lambs. They didn't come too close to him at first and their mothers watched him suspiciously, ready to butt him with their heads if need be. He managed to find his lamb, the one he had rescued, and to get close enough to stroke it. Its fleece was thicker, its body sturdier.

'Haven't you grown?'

He wasn't sure which of the others was the one he had seen born. Maybe the smallest one, maybe not. Maybe that one had come afterwards.

From the corner of his eye he saw her leave the barn at last and return to the cottage. He climbed back over the gate and went to knock on the kitchen door.

'Hi.'

'Hi. Come in.'

'Shall I take my shoes off?'

'No, they're not too bad.'

'The cake smells nice. I mean, not that I was expecting any...' He felt himself blush.

'It's just cooling. I'll cut it in a moment.' She smiled. 'How's your lamb?'

'Fine, great.'

He almost asked her how long it would be before the lambs got sent to the market, but he decided that he didn't really want to know, not today.

The electric kettle hissed, then clicked as it turned itself off.

'Tea?'

'Thanks.'

She didn't offer him any Coke and he didn't like to ask. He would have preferred it, but tea was all right.

As she made the tea and sliced the cake, he glanced around the kitchen. It was littered with correspondence: letters, feed bills and unopened envelopes.

On one of them he saw her name.

Ms A. Starne.

He stared at it, wondering why the surname was familiar, where he had seen it before.

'Sugar?'

'Er, no thanks.'

'Milk though?'

'Thanks, yes.'

Then he remembered. In the churchyard, there amongst the headstones, the smallest of them all – the one commemorating the briefest of the lives which lay there, that of Matthew Starne, who had lived for only one day.

Was it her son? Or was it just a coincidence? Or the child of a relative perhaps?

She poured out the tea and cut a decent-sized slab of cake for him.

'Here. Boys are always hungry – isn't that right?'

'Well…'

He accepted the slice of cake and bit into it. It was still warm.

How could he ask her? Maybe the grave in the churchyard had nothing to do with her.

'It's Joe, isn't it?'

'Yes, that's right.'

'I don't get many visitors.'

'It's quite a lonely spot.'

'Oh, I don't mind that.'

'Nice though.'

'Well, it is when the sun's shining.'

Now what to say? He didn't know. How did you go about it? How did you steer things around to what you really wanted to say, without being too abrupt about it and doing it all wrong.

He coughed to clear his throat.

'Don't forget – you can call me Anna,' she said.

He'd been wondering about that – if it would still be all right to use her name. He was glad of the permission.

'Anna…'

'Yes?'

'Would you mind if I asked you something?'

She smiled, as if amused, but not in any malicious way.

'Have you ever lost anyone?'

She took a moment to answer.

'Lost anyone? In what way?'

He looked down at the plate, at the cake, the crumbs.

'Do you remember the boy who vanished?'

'Vanished?'

'A while back … a couple of years ago…?'

She nodded.

'I was with him … the morning he went. He was my friend … my best friend … my only real friend really.'

'I see.'

'Have you ever lost anyone?'

She stiffened.

'Why do you ask?'

'Because I don't think anybody understands. I don't think they know what it means.'

'Maybe they do, but you just don't see it.'

He shook his head.

'I don't think they understand at all. You see, I was the last to see him. I should have said something. I should have told him not to go or I should have stopped him. If I had, none of it would have happened. And then, afterwards, I left it a couple of days before I told anyone about it – because I'd promised not to tell on him.'

'Could you have stopped him? Would he have listened to you?'

He shrugged. 'I don't know. But I could have tried.'

'But how could you have known what was going to happen?'

'I don't know. I just feel I should have done.'

'But that's impossible. You can't blame yourself.'

He wanted to ask her about the stone in the cemetery, or maybe for her to volunteer the information herself, so he wouldn't have to. But she didn't.

'Anna…'

'Hmm?'

'Do you believe that people can come back?'

'Come back? What do you mean, Joe? Come back in what way?'

'I don't know … I suppose I mean … if not in one way … then another. You know some people believe that when people die ... they sort of live on ... in another place ... and you can talk to them.'

'Talk to them?' The way she said it, full of incredulity, made him realise how different she was from all the other adults around, from Frea and Ran, from his mother and all her friends. They all inhabited this world of weirdness really. There was nothing practical about it. Anna, on the other hand, was all practicality and common sense. 'How can you talk to people who aren't there?'

'Well, get in touch with them then.'

'How?'

'Well...' He felt his face colour. 'You know ... with their spirits ... and things.'

'Ah.'

She went and got herself more tea. She offered him some, but he shook his head. 'You mean seances – things like that?'

He nodded. 'Yes, I suppose,' he said. 'I mean, I'm not saying I believe in it, I just wondered if you did. Because I thought, you see, if there was any truth in it – that people could, you know, communicate with people who were dead – well, couldn't you also ... communicate with the living?'

She looked at him with wry amusement.

'Couldn't you just phone them up?' she said. 'Even I've got a mobile and I'm not exactly at the cutting edge.'

'I meant ... if they had vanished ... had gone ... and you didn't know where ... maybe somehow ... you could get in touch with them.'

She sat down opposite him at the table. He felt that if she had known him better she would have taken his hand.

'Joe,' she said, 'you know what I think ... I think that people are never entirely lost to us ... we find them even after they have gone, all around us, in so many things. You can find them in all kinds of places, all kinds of ways … in music … memories … just looking out of the window and seeing the sun go down … in other people … gestures … sounds. They're always there, one way or another.'

He sipped his tea. He drank it carefully, afraid of slurping it and her thinking he had no manners.

'Do you think,' he said, 'that I'll ever find him?'

'I don't know, Joe.'

'Do you think that he's still alive?'

She didn't answer.

'I think I'm going to ask him that,' he said.

'You're going to ask him? How?'

'I've got a board at home that spells out words.'

She didn't seem as if she altogether approved.

'I see.'

'Only I don't have anyone to do it with.'

'Do your mother and father know?'

'I don't have a father any more. He's gone.'

'I think you ought to talk to your mother about it, Joe.'

'I can't. She wouldn't understand.'

'You'd be surprised. Try her.'

'I already did.'

There was an old-fashioned clock on the window ledge, the kind you wound up with a large key. The clock ticked heavily and slowly, filling the kitchen with its languid notification of the passage of time.

Some feelings you could never describe. They were like colours without names. They fell between other colours and blurred into indefinability. All you could say was that they were there in the slant of the sunlight or the atmosphere of a room; in a scent or a sound, in a gesture or a motion; they were there in a landscape or in the architecture of a house. You would feel them, and they would vanish and never return for years and years, until the things that had created them suddenly recombined, and then you would experience them again, and they would all but break your heart. Then they would be gone again, maybe this time forever, like the heron flying across the fields, or the snow geese going home.

There were feelings that there weren't any names for, not in all the languages in the world.

Joe wished more than anything that he could tell somebody how he felt, that he could finally tell somebody how it was to be him, to be the only one still believing, who would always believe. But he couldn't. It was impossible. The words did not exist.

He saw the time on the clock.

'I ought to be going, Anna.'

'Yes of course. Me too – must get back to work.'

'Thanks for the cake.'

She stood, clearing up, bustling and businesslike, taking cups and plates to the sink.

'You're very welcome, Joe.'

'Sorry I took up so much of your time.'

'Not at all. Glad of the company.'

He took his bike helmet and headed for the door.

'I shan't bother you again,' he said. 'I shan't come back.'

'Joe…'

'I'm a nuisance.'

'You are not a nuisance. Come back soon and see the lambs.'

'You sure?'

'Of course I'm sure. If I wasn't sure I wouldn't ask you.'

'Thanks then.'

'You're welcome.'

She watched from the cottage as he got back on his bike and headed down the road. He waved and she waved in return. He sped on, feeling as if some great weight had been taken from him, feeling alive and even happy – something he hadn't felt for a long time.

She went back inside and closed the door behind her. She had a couple of things to take down to the cellar and then she would need to go out and see to the hens. Then there was a fence to repair and she had to change the oil in the Land Rover. That was life, work without end. But better it should be that way than empty and raw. It was good to keep busy, it was easier. She'd always found it better that way, to be occupied, to have your hands full. It took your mind off all kinds of things, and then they no longer bothered you.

Chapter 13

Thirst

Impatient as he was to return, he did not go that way the following week, but left it until the Saturday after. This time he was disappointed to see that there really was nobody there. The Land Rover was not parked outside in the yard, and though he went and peered into the garage, it was not there either.

He lingered a while, hoping that she might return, but trying to make it look as though he had just arrived, so that if she did come back she wouldn't guess that he had been waiting. The minutes passed, became a quarter then a half hour. Still she didn't come.

He looked back along the road. If the Land Rover was coming he would see it a good mile away. In the other direction there was a slight incline as the road rose up towards the village.

He went and looked at the lambs anyway. He walked through the yard, with the hens scattering; some of the geese hissed at him to go away, but they didn't attack. He climbed over the five-barred gate and wandered amid the small flock of sheep. As he stood there, he heard the sound of an engine, but it wasn't a car, it was the small-engine sound of a microlight aircraft. He looked up as the tiny, kite-like plane and its dangling pilot went by overhead. He waved and the man waved back at him. A few minutes later the sound had gone.

He walked back to the yard and strolled around the outbuildings. He even tried the door to the kitchen, to see if it was locked. It was. He wondered if he would have gone in, had he found it open. He told himself that he wouldn't, but he knew that he would.

The farm still had the look about it of faint dilapidation. He guessed that she did as much as anyone could, but that she never had quite enough money.

Now he was alone there, he felt that there was something strange about the place, then he realised that it was the sense of not being alone, of being watched.

He scanned slowly around the yard, trying to quell his unease, only to find himself staring into two huge eyes – it was one of the horses, peering out at him from the stable near the barn. He went over and stroked its nose and wished he had an apple to give it, or a sugar lump.

It must be so lonely here, he thought. In the middle of the week. In the quiet of the long winter darkness, when the days were over almost as soon as they had begun. You wondered that anyone could stand such isolation for long – that they would choose it as a way to live.

Once again he had that feeling of being watched, of being listened to. It wasn't the horse, it was something else.

For one terrible, sickening moment, he realised that she might have a camera, a security camera, up on the corner of the barn, staring down at him right now, recording his every movement. It would have captured his arrival, his knock at the door, his looking into the garage, his climbing over the gate to the field where the lambs were kept … his trying the kitchen door.

Oh no. If it had recorded that. Him trying the door. He'd never be able to come back now, never. She'd come home and replay the tape and there he would be, wandering around her property, trying the door to her house…

No, it was all right. He looked all around, but there was no camera. She didn't have the money for cameras and elaborate – or even basic – security systems.

He made his way over the yard, towards the grid and road. Still the feeling pursued him. He sensed that there was someone right behind him, reaching out to touch his shoulder. He swivelled round, heart drumming, fists up, ready to fight.

'What do you want?'

Nobody there.

Caw, caw, caw.

Two rooks left their branches and took off into the air. They flew on over the fields, their cries seeming to mock him for being so nervous. He hurried to his bike and quickly rode away. He didn't look back, not until he had reached the village. He didn't go to sit in the churchyard today either, but remained outside, perched on the wall.

There was a wedding that afternoon. When they emerged from the church he came down from the wall, so as not to get in the way of their photographs. They didn't sound like country people. Their voices and manners came from the city. They had probably wanted a picturesque wedding, that was all, in a small village church.

Maybe, he thought, Anna was among the guests. That would explain her absence from the farm. He looked for her, wondering what she would look like out of her uniform of wellingtons, green waxed jacket and blue muddy jeans. But she wasn't there.

He finished his chocolate bar and set off for home.

'Good bike ride?' his mother asked him when she came in.

'Fine,' he said. 'Fine.'

He never said any more than that and he never told her where he had been. Even when she asked he wouldn't tell her – or rather he wouldn't tell her the truth. Everyone was entitled to their secrets, even if only to prove by having them that you were getting older, you were growing up, you were somebody with a life of your own outside the four walls of home.

'Joseph,' she said that night, maybe feeling intuitively that it was a question she needed to ask. 'You don't think about it so much now, do you?'

'Think about what?' he said.

'The disappearance. About Jonah.'

He said what she wanted to hear.

'No ... not so much.'

She nodded.

'We have to rebuild,' she said, 'and move on. It doesn't mean you have to forget. It just means making a new life and accepting what's happened. It's not a matter of forgetting ... it's rebuilding. Ran thinks so too,' she added.

Does he now? Joe thought. So you've been discussing it with him? Which is all very well, only I don't actually think that Ran is the fount of all wisdom. I think he's a deluded poser and an idiot.

The trouble was that Joe could never forget and never forgive himself for his delay in reporting what he knew. If he had come forward earlier they might have found Jonah. Those wasted hours might have made all the difference.

What his mother didn't understand was that he was responsible; he still was, and always would be.

The following Saturday he rode back to the farm. This time he carried a small rucksack. Inside it was the board.

Jonah was torn now, between going on and turning back. If he turned back, he'd at least know how long it was going to take him. The trouble was he'd come a long, long way. It was a good two hours now since he had started, must have been. So if he turned around now that would be another two hours before he got anything to drink. He was absolutely parched. If it got any worse he'd have to risk the water in the ditch, green slime or no green slime. Whereas if he went on...

A village might be around the next corner.

So he went on to see.

But around the next corner was another corner and another after that.

Then at last there was another road – a crossroads – and a sign that a village was little more than a mile away, if he went in the right direction.

Only thing was...

Someone had twisted the post around. He could tell because the arms were all off true. They weren't exactly pointing at the roads at all.

Maybe someone had done it because they were drunk one night, or because they didn't like townies and wanted them to get lost. Maybe they did it just for the hellof it.

Maybe they did it because they were afraid that little green aliens were going to land among the corn circles in flying saucers, and this would confuse them and send them packing.

But which way to take?

Left or right? One way was to the village, one and a quarter miles away. The other was a seven-mile loop back to the town he had come from. Or he could just go back the way he had come or straight on.

A mile and a quarter. He could do that in fifteen, twenty minutes. Then there would be a village shop, with a nice big chiller cabinet in it, full of cans and bottles of cold Coke and juice.

Left or right then? Heads or tails?

He guessed the road sign was roughly correct, despite being askew. His inner compass told him to trust his instincts. So he turned to the right and headed on for the village, speeding up despite his thirst.

He walked for twenty minutes, but the village did not appear. He must have been walking slower than he thought – or the mile and a quarter was a serious underestimate. The twenty minutes turned into half an hour. He stopped to wipe the sweat from his face. His T-shirt was sticking to his back. His thirst was raging.

He'd come the wrong way. The sign had been wrong. It was half an hour back to the crossroads now and another half an hour maybe to the village.

He felt close to tears. He wasn't just thirsty now, he was hungry and aching, dizzy and weak. He sat down by the roadside on a fallen branch. He could be sitting in school now, looking out of the window as the teacher's voice lulled him into daydreams. He could be thinking about the fire engine that had screamed past and what he might have found if he had run after it – flames and smoke, charred bodies even and a house on fire.

But no. Daydreaming wasn't good enough. It never was for him. He always had to go and do the thing that you really only ought to think of doing and not actually do at all. Others talked and others wished, but Jonah was the one with the nerve, the one who actually went and did it.

He had a reputation to live up to.

It was his own fault, but he'd get back eventually. Stupid fire engine. Stupid fire. If there was a fire. And there probably wasn't. It was being so thirsty, that was all. He wouldn't mind the hunger and the heat and the ache in his legs, if only he wasn't so thirsty.

A few more steps then. Just in case he was wrong. Only as far as the brow of the hill. Maybe the village was just over there. Maybe it just seemed further than it actually was because of the heat. Only a few more steps. Get to the top, take a look. If it wasn't there he would turn back and start the long trek home.

Maybe he could suck a stone. That was supposed to help thirst, wasn't it? He'd seen it in a film. And he had a book – about surviving in adverse conditions. Told you what to do if attacked by crocodiles as well. Useful book that.

Trouble was, you'd want a clean stone. You wouldn't want to suck any old pebble – it might be covered in germs. Or a dog might have done something on it and how would you tell?

What you'd really need would be some water to wash it with first. But then, if you had some water, you could drink it and you'd not need to suck the stone to keep your thirst at bay anyhow.

That was the trouble with this survival stuff. It was a whole lot more complicated than they made out. In fact, that was the trouble with life itself – it was never quite what you'd expected.

Anyway, maybe he was on the right road after all. Maybe the village shop with the ice-cold cans inside would be just over the brow of…

It wasn't. There was no village, no shop, no nothing. He'd gone the wrong way. Someone had twisted the sign right round back at the crossroads.

Nothing for it then, he had to go back. He paused at the brow of the hill, his T-shirt saturated with sweat where the backpack rested on it. He was just about to turn around when he saw something.

His salvation.

Yes!

There it was. That would do it.

He hurried on, actually breaking into a jog now in his rush to get there.

A few more metres, a few more minutes…

His problems would all be over.

Chapter 14

Question...

If Joe could have followed Jonah's footsteps, it would have solved it all. If there had been any real footsteps to follow. In a certain sense that was what he had tried to do for a long time now – to follow some faint, near-indiscernible trail. But all it had led to was a blank wall – to the end of an unfamiliar alleyway, and then...

Puff!

Vanished like smoke.

On the other hand, maybe Jonah *was* still there, a ghostly, guiding presence, influencing him in ways he didn't know, directing his steps and urging him onwards...

This way, Joe. Follow this road to find me. I'll be waiting, there at the end. You'll find me and you'll know then, and everything will be revealed.

...like a hand moving the tumbler towards the letters on the board, spelling out the words it could not say.

Perhaps that unseen hand guided Joe, making him take this road and not another. Maybe destiny was behind every impulse and the route had all been worked out, well in advance. He moved from letter to letter, and finally the letters would make a word, or a series of words. They would spell out the answer.

You have found me.

Here I am.

Joe reached the farm. Anna was out in the field, driving the tractor. When she saw him she waved and cut the engine. She climbed down from the cab and walked to the cottage. He left his bike and met her by the door.

'Hello, stranger.'

'Hello, Anna.'

He didn't know why she'd called him a stranger. It had only been a few weeks, surely. And it wasn't his fault. He'd been back the weekend before and she hadn't been there. Was it his fault if she went away? It didn't make him a stranger.

'I came by last week, actually…'

He wished he hadn't said that. He hadn't meant to. It might seem like snooping.

'Oh, I wasn't here.'

'I know. I knocked on the door.'

'You should have left a note.'

'Didn't think of it … anyway, I didn't have a pen or paper.'

'Come in.'

The door was unlocked. She pushed it open, then paused.

'Actually, when you came by last week … did you hear anything?'

He watched her.

'Hear anything?'

'Anything strange?'

He remembered his sense of foreboding, his feeling that there had been somebody following him across the yard; he remembered how he had turned to confront them, heart pounding, fists at the ready.

'No, no … nothing at all. Why?'

'Oh, no reason. It's just sometimes … I don't know … I think I hear something.'

'What sort of thing do you hear?'

'I don't know.' She looked back towards where the tractor stood – at the empty Levels and the sprawling fields. 'It sounds like a voice sometimes … muffled … far away … it's probably just the wind in the hedges. It can sound almost human sometimes.'

'I know what you mean. I hear it when I'm cycling.'

'Just the wind, probably. Come on in.'

He went inside with her. There was no cake cooling on the window ledge today. She opened a packet of biscuits and spilled them out on to a plate.

'Help yourself.'

'Thanks.'

She filled the kettle.

'I brought it,' he said.

He was disappointed to see that she looked bewildered. She had obviously forgotten.

'The board,' he said.

He shrugged off his backpack and put it down on the table.

'The board?'

'The one I made. That I told you about.'

She remembered now.

'Oh, right. You brought it for me to see?'

She still seemed a little confused about something, not quite getting the point. He'd rated her a bit higher than that too. For an adult she had seemed quite perceptive, not to need any explanations. Maybe she was tired today. He guessed she worked too hard. She'd probably been up since five.

'Well, not just to see… '

She understood him now. She didn't look that happy about it either. He busied himself opening the board and showing her the good job he had made of it.

'I modelled it on one in the shop.'

'What shop?'

'Mystic Moments – it's where my mother works. They sell all this mystic stuff. Crystal balls and tarot cards and hash pipes – though I'm not supposed to know what they're for. I'm supposed to think they're for blowing bubbles.'

'I see.'

'It's a good copy.'

'I'm sure it is.'

'I didn't make a pointer though. We just need a tumbler … a small glass … do you have one?'

'Look, Joe…' she said.

'There's nothing to be afraid of,' he said.

'No, it's not that.'

'Please,' he said. 'Please do it with me.'

He could see she was against it; she either didn't care for or didn't believe in that kind of thing.

But she could tell how much it meant to him, how important it had become.

She sighed. 'OK. I suppose there's no harm in trying it once. But once only. Please don't ask again.'

'Thanks.'

'So what happens?'

'Have you got the tumbler?'

She fetched one and joined him at the table.

'Put it here – upside down.'

'And then?'

'The atmosphere has to be right.'

'How's that done?'

'Do you have any incense?'

'No.'

'Joss sticks? Scented candles?'

'Well, I've got some candles for when the power goes – plain, ordinary ones.'

'That'll have to do.'

She fetched a packet of candles from the drawer.

'I suppose I ought to draw the curtains then – for the atmosphere to be right?'

'Please.'

'OK.' She sighed again, a patient, long-suffering sigh. She lit two candles, shook the match out, then drew the curtains. 'Right. Now what?' She sat back down at the table.

'We get in the mood. Just sit quietly for a moment.'

'All right.'

They sat, silent. The clock helped. He had forgotten the clock. It was better than incense. Its loud, heavy sound seemed to stroke the air, smooth it down, as if running a hand along the fur of a cat. There, there. Calm and quiet. Just the purr of the fridge, the tick of the clock, the light of the flickering candles.

He reached out and touched the top of the upturned glass with his finger. He nodded at Anna to do the same.

'Now what?' She spoke in a whisper. She sounded apprehensive.

'Just wait.' He was whispering too.

They waited. The room seemed to fill with a presence, invisible but strong.

'Is anyone there?' His voice was barely audible.

Slowly the glass began to move. It slid across the board to the top left-hand corner.

Yes.

Yes.

He swallowed. His mouth was dry.

'Is it Jonah?'

The glass moved again, across to the right.

No.

'Who is it?'

At first the glass did not move. Then it started to slide. It moved and stopped at the letter M. It remained there and did not move on.

His mouth was so dry now he could barely speak. His words came out as a rasp, a dry croak.

'Do you know Jonah?' he asked.

The glass moved to *Yes*.

'Is Jonah dead?' he said.

The glass began to move again, to the top right-hand corner.

No.

It stopped at No.

Joe glanced across at Anna. Her skin was pale in the glow of the candlelight, her face tense, her eyes staring. Then his heart began to pound, his breath came fast and shallow, his vision grew dim; there was just the board and the candles, yellow pinpricks in his field of sight.

'Are *you* dead?' he asked.

The glass began to move to the left. But then it was as if a third hand of enormous strength had taken hold of the tumbler; it seized it and slid it with all its might. The glass went flying, clean off the board and right off the table, smashing into fragments against the metal stove.

'Oh my god!'

Anna was up on her feet. She looked panicked and terrified.

'What was it? What did that!'

She hurried to the window and pulled back the curtains, letting sunlight into the room.

'Never bring that thing here again, Joe. You hear me? Never!'

'I'm sorry. I didn't know. I didn't mean it to happen. I'm sorry.'

He was already down on his knees, trying to pick up the broken glass, to make it all right.

'*Leave it!*'

Her voice startled him. It had completely changed – abrupt and angry.

'You'll cut yourself...'

Then she was calm, herself again. She'd only been angry because she had been concerned for him.

'Here, let me get a pan and a brush.'

She fetched them, along with some old newspaper, and between them they found all the pieces they could and cleared everything up.

'Might still be some small bits,' Joe warned. 'I wouldn't go barefoot.'

'Thank you. Now put that board back in the bag and we'll have some tea and then go look at the lambs.'

'OK.'

He could tell that she didn't want to discuss what had happened – though it was all he wanted to talk about.

Alive. Jonah was still alive. If a glass moving across a board could be believed.

But the way it had broken, the way it had been hurled across the room...

'Are *you* dead?'

The glass had been moving towards the left corner of the board, to the word Yes. But some power had stopped it. It had smashed the glass into pieces. It would not allow M to be dead. It would never, ever be able to admit even the possibility of such a thing, and it would not be contradicted.

Anna wrapped up the last of the broken glass and dropped the folded newspaper into the bin.

'There,' she said. 'It's done now.'

Joe saw that her hand was shaking.

Chapter 15

And Answer

Joe wanted to tell somebody, but there was no one who would listen, at least not in the way he would want them to – with an open mind and with understanding, not with criticism, or incredulity, or disapproval.

He even thought of going to the police, but what could he tell them? What would he say when he approached the counter of the police station?

'Excuse me, but you remember that boy who went missing…? Well, I happen to have a home-made Ouija board here, which informs me, on the highest possible authority, that he is actually still alive and…'

Somehow he didn't think so.

He should have asked it where Jonah was. He should have pressed it, like one of those interviewers trying to pin a politician down on the evening news, insisting it answer the question. If he wasn't dead, where was he then? If only Joe had thought of that.

Wise after the event again, same as ever. Somehow he always thought of the right thing to do when it was too late to do it.

It was like having money that you couldn't spend – important, vital information that you somehow couldn't do anything with. In a way he was no better off than he had been. He had never believed Jonah to be dead anyway. He alone had kept the torch burning and the flame alive.

As time passed he felt disappointed and resentful – even cheated. The glass moving around the board had seemed to tell him something significant, but it all amounted to nothing in the end.

Unless…

He went back to the board, sitting alone in his room with one of his mother's joss sticks burning and with the curtains drawn. But nothing happened. It didn't seem to work on your own.

'Joseph! What are you doing up there?'

His mother's anxiety shattered his concentration.

'Nothing, Mum – homework.'

'You aren't playing with matches, are you?'

'No!'

As if he would. Who, in their right mind, played with matches? Then again, if she had known what he was up to, she'd have gone all dramatic and told him he *was* playing with fire. That sort of thing was best left to those who knew what they were doing, she'd have said. People like Ran, no doubt, who looked and dressed the part. Of course, if he shaved his beard off and put on a suit he'd look about as spiritual as a traffic warden. It was just clothes, not even skin deep.

Joe toyed with the idea of asking somebody else – somebody from school, but he couldn't think of anybody he could confide in or who would take it seriously enough. There was only Anna, really, and she had told him not to come back with the Ouija board, so that option was out. Unless he could talk her round, of course. Maybe she would even have become intrigued. Left alone to think about it, she might want to know more.

He'd leave it a week and then go back there. He wouldn't take the board with him, but he'd sound her out. Maybe she would have changed her mind.

'Would you like me to come with you? I could probably get the afternoon off.'

'No, it's OK, thanks.'

His mother coming with him was the very last thing he wanted.

'Don't you ever feel like some company sometimes?'

'No, I'm fine.'

'Don't you ever get lonely?'

'No. I like being on my own. I don't have to keep up with anybody and they don't have to keep up with me.'

That was the best thing about being on your own – you did everything just as you wanted to, you travelled at your own speed. There was no compromise, no getting annoyed either, with other people and their differences. And anyway, solitude wasn't necessarily loneliness; they were two different things.

'I worry about you sometimes, Joe.'

'Well, you don't have to, Mum. I'm fine.'

'OK, well, if you're sure then.'

'I'm fine. I said I was fine.'

'What time will you be back?'

'Usual time.'

'OK. Where do you think you'll go?'

'Oh, I don't know…' He knew perfectly well, but he wasn't telling her any more than he had to. 'Just out on the Levels somewhere. One of my routes.'

'OK then. Well, you've got your phone. It is charged up, isn't it?'

'Of course it's charged up. You're the one who forgets to charge their phone up, Mum – or I ring you and half the time it's not turned on.'

'Yes, well, just as long as it's in your pocket. Don't lose it, will you?'

'Mum, for crying out—'

In one ear, out the other. She just didn't listen to him. She was getting worse too. He wondered if it wouldn't be better if she met somebody – another man. It wouldn't be ideal, of course, especially if he moved in with them, as it would be someone else to get used to, but it might do her some good. She hadn't been out with anybody, he didn't think, since they had split up and his father had left for India.

'OK, well, I'll see you later,' he said.

'I'll cook tea for about half six or seven.'

She left for the shop. He checked his bike over, wheeled it outside, and locked up the house. He put on his gloves and bike helmet and set off down the road.

The wheels knew the way. They made the decisions at the junctions and crossroads. All he had to do was turn the pedals and the wheels would do the rest. Perhaps that was how to do it – to somehow let his mind grow empty and let chance and destiny carry him, guided perhaps by Jonah's invisible hand.

This way now, this way, my friend.

He could hear the sound again of the fire engine approaching, he could hear Jonah's voice: 'Come on! Let's follow it! Let's find the fire!'

He could see Jonah pelting off down the road. He could hear himself calling after him, 'No, no, we'll be late for school!' And he had been late, far too late. He could hear the engine and see Jonah running after it, like it was the Pied Piper of Hamelin.

There had been one child left in that story. He hadn't been able to follow the Piper because he was lame, unable to run after the enticing sound. Just like me, Joe thought. He'd always been a little like that – crippled by inhibitions and worries, never entirely spontaneous in anything he did.

He'd never been like Jonah. He could never just run after the Piper because he loved the sound. But today, at least, it felt different. Today, he felt carried along.

Everything seemed faster today – his progress across the Levels, the way the turning wheels ate up the miles. Then there was Anna, out in the fields, mending fences, mud on her hands and her hair in her eyes. He called. She waved to him. He turned off the road. It was almost a formula, there was no need to question why or how it worked. It followed a track, moved like a train along a steel road.

'Do you want to see the lambs?'

'Yes, can I?'

'They're growing now. They soon won't be lambs any more. Here, wait, let's have some cake first.'

And there it was, cooling on the sill, with a muslin cloth draped over it, to keep off the insects. Just like in the old days, the ones you read about in picture books when you were small, though you had never known them yourself.

She'd been expecting him. That was why she had baked the cake. There was an old song about that: *If I'd known you were coming, I'd have baked a cake*. Yet there had been a cake cooling on the sill the very first time he had come.

Maybe she had been expecting him, even back then. Maybe she had always been expecting him.

'Anna…'

'Yes?'

'Can I ask you something? About the village?'

'The village?'

'In the churchyard there.'

She looked at him, her face suddenly hard, the small muscles at the side of her jaw clenching tight.

'Yes?'

'I go there sometimes … just to sit on the bench, I mean … and, well, sometimes I look at the stones too.'

'Why?' she asked. 'What for? I mean, at your age…'

'I just wonder,' he said, 'about all the people who have gone … I like to look at their names and see how old-fashioned they are, and to see their dates and to work out how long they had, and to see how all the things change over the years – like what people put on the headstones, the poems and the psalms.'

'I see.'

'Some people had such long lives, but some people hardly had any time at all. There's a stone there for a baby. He only lived one day.'

'I know,' she said. 'I know.'

'And I noticed that you had the same name … same surname…'

She turned her eyes away from him and looked out of the window at the faraway hills.

'Yes,' she said. 'That's right.'

'I just wanted to say … that I'm sorry … that I was sorry … that was all.'

She turned back to look at him.

'Thank you, Joe,' she said. 'That's very kind of you … but there's no need … it's like you said once, I don't know if you remember … about people coming back … you asked if they came back…'

'That's right.'

'I think maybe they do. You don't always recognise them at first. But then you see something in someone and you realise … it's almost as if they'd come back to you … the person you had lost.'

'Yes…'

He didn't understand her. But it didn't matter. He'd said what he had wanted to say and she knew that he knew and that he was sorry that it had happened to her, and that she had had such a loss in her life.

'Can I go and see the lambs now?' he said.

'Sure,' she nodded. 'Of course you can. Watch out for the big ewe. She's taken to butting people.'

He left the kitchen. She remained there, gathering up the cups and plates, wiping up crumbs. He crossed to the field, climbed the gate – which was less trouble than opening it – and went to look at the lambs.

148

'His' lamb was in a far corner, as distinctive as ever, with its black face and mottled fleece like a two-tone coat – a small Pied Piper itself.

It was too fat to squeeze under any gates now or to drop through any cattle grids. At that moment it was ignoring the grass and the feed troughs and was rooting around in a huge compost pile in a far corner of the field, trying to burrow into the base of it and pull something out.

'Hello! How are you? What are you doing in there? You're not a pig, you know!'

The lamb raised its head apprehensively at Joe's approach. On the one hand it wanted to run away; on the other, it might have found something good to eat.

'Hey, what've you got there? What's that?'

The lamb ran off. It was plainly the nervous type – or else what it had found wasn't edible. It scampered off to another part of the field and started chewing some grass. Life for a sheep was one long meal.

Disappointed that the lamb wouldn't come to him and suffer being stroked, Joe was about to return to the cottage when curiosity propelled him forward. What had the lamb found? What had it half dragged out from the heap?

He went to it and looked down. It lay there, still almost totally buried under the compost. It must have lain there, unnoticed, for ages, the cuttings and decaying leaves piling up on top of it.

All he saw at first was a strap, there at the very bottom of the pile. He stepped nearer, curious, and crouched down to examine it more closely. He tugged at it, then he yanked at it harder until finally it came out.

It was a backpack. Like the one he used to have a couple of years ago. He'd got a new one since. The old one had worn out.

This was just the same as his old one. Identical. Same colour – or it had been once – same style, same logo.

There was only one person he knew who'd had a backpack like that.

Jonah.

It was Jonah's. It was Jonah's backpack.

No, that was ridiculous. How could it be?

The zip was plastic, so it hadn't rusted. The bag itself was damp and mildewed and stank to high heaven. Had it been cotton or canvas, instead of some man-made acrylic, it would have rotted into nothing by now. But, other than the dirt and damp and the stains from the compost, it wasn't in bad condition. He zipped the top open and looked inside. There it was, Jonah's name, written on the inside in indelible ink.

Steal this and you die!
Jonah Byford.

There was still an exercise book inside – sodden now, and the ink had run. But you could just make out the name on the front. It was his. *It was his.*

He had found it! Something tangible at last, some concrete proof. Jonah had been here. He had passed this way. It was a clue – a clue! One that the police had never found. They'd probably never even searched here. Not this place, not every little bit. Why would they? It wasn't a man who was running the place. There was nothing suspicious here.

At last he had something. All the days and months – all the hope he had never relinquished, all the belief he had never abandoned when everyone else had given up. He had been so alone in his faith and his certainty. Now here it was at last – a real, tangible clue; undeniable evidence.

Joe felt both shattered and triumphant – afraid but excited. And vindicated too. He had been right all along.

He had to tell someone immediately, show them the trophy, let the world know that here was evidence of Jonah – maybe even proof of his continuing existence.

He turned and ran back to the farmhouse, shouting out her name.

'Anna! Look, Anna!'

Wait till he told her. Wait till she saw.

He waved the backpack as he ran.

'Anna! Anna! Look!'

He scrambled over the gate and sprinted through the rutted mud of the yard. His phone fell from his pocket. Never mind. He'd come back for it. This was far more important now.

'Anna, look! Anna, I've found him! I have!'

Well, he hadn't of course, but it felt like it. That would come next, very soon.

In his excitement and triumph he forgot to ask himself one vital question – exactly *how* the backpack could ever have got *there*. Who would have deliberately buried it deep under a huge pile of rotting vegetation? Had that person expected it also to rot away?

Maybe someone had simply dropped it, or thrown it over the fence into the field as they passed, and it had lain there unnoticed for years as the cuttings and the waste and the leaves piled on top of it. Maybe. Or maybe not.

She squinted out of the window and saw him running, the bag held high like a victor's trophy. He burst in through the kitchen door, going so fast he couldn't stop immediately and almost careered into the far wall.

'Anna, look!' He was breathless. 'It's … the backpack … it's Jonah's. He must have come this way. We must ring the police and tell them. They might be able to find him now. It might say where he's gone! Don't you think, Anna? Anna…?'

The strange thing was that she didn't look pleased at all. She seemed to share not one fragment of his joy. If anything she looked sad – angry and sad. And she said the most peculiar thing.

'You had to find that, didn't you, Joseph? You just had to find it. You couldn't leave things alone, could you?'

He was perplexed as to why she was calling him Joseph and not Joe – just the way his mother did when she was angry with him, or about to broach a difficult subject.

Anna seemed angry with him too.

Then he realised that she was turning the key in the lock and, before he could make sense of it, she was reaching up to where the shotgun was kept and she had broken it open and put a cartridge into the barrel. Then she snapped it shut and released the safety catch.

'You just had to find it, didn't you. When it was all going so well.'

Chapter 16

Matthew

The thirst was worse than ever and he was just going to have to do something about it no matter what. Even the ditch water would be preferable to this. You saw programmes about Africa and people with flies in their eyes and you wondered why they didn't wash them out, and why they drank the water they did, which gave them river blindness and parasites and intestinal worms.

Then you got thirsty and you found out. They drank it because there was no alternative.

But even then Jonah might have thought twice about it. Even with the terrible thirst and all the rest, he still might have turned back rather than go on further. No doubt he would have done, had it been a man standing there in the yard of the smallholding. But it wasn't, it was a woman. So he could trust her. Women were safe, women were nice. The strangers they warned you about were always men, even when they didn't say so explicitly. You knew without them telling you that the stranger to be afraid of was a man.

She put the hose down and went to turn off the tap. The arc of water seemed to magnify his thirst. She walked towards the gate. He made his way over to her.

'Hi...'

She stopped, looked at him strangely, then smiled.

'Matthew,' she said. 'It's you. At last.'

'Um ... Jonah actually,' he mumbled, but he didn't want to correct her too much as she seemed so friendly

*and he really did want a drink of water. Or maybe she
even had some Coke in the fridge. And possibly a
home-made, rich farmhouse fruitcake, or some
biscuits and a plate of scones.*

'I'm sorry to bother you, but I'm a little lost...'

'No, not at all.'

*Only she didn't seem to mean, 'No, you're not
bothering me.' She seemed to be correcting him, to be
saying, 'No, you're* not *lost.'*

'I'm really thirsty, and I was wondering...'

*'Of course you can. Come in. You took such a long
time to get here.'*

*He didn't really understand that one either. How
would she have known how long it had taken him to
get there? It wasn't as if she had been expecting him.*

'This way, Matthew...'

'No, it's Jonah actually...'

'Come into the house. Everything's ready.'

Everything's ready? *Maybe she had been cooking some
lunch, and had just popped out to hose the yard, and
now the meal was ready. Well, that was fine, because he
wasn't just thirsty – there were some big pangs of hunger
there too. Maybe it would be pie or pizza, or she'd been
baking some potatoes and had enough to share.*

*He followed her across the yard. She turned and
smiled. She seemed to have taken an instant liking to
him. Which was good.*

*She held the door open for him to go inside. He
hesitated just for a second, wondering if he was doing
the right thing. But she looked so kind and pretty
almost ... she reminded him of photographs of his
mother when she'd been holding him in her arms.*

*'You look just like I thought you would,' she said as
he walked past her and into the house.*

*He didn't know what she meant, but he still wasn't
worried. He had such a thirst now. He went straight to*

the tap and turned it on. She appeared at his side with a tumbler.

'Thanks.'

He took it from her and filled it, then drank down the water in hurried gulps.

'Whoa, whoa, not so fast, Matthew.'

He wished she wouldn't call him Matthew. He'd already told her twice that his name was Jonah, but clearly she hadn't been listening.

'Careful,' she said, 'or you'll choke.'

He refilled the glass, emptied it, drank a third glass, then placed it down on the drainer.

'Well, thank you. Thanks very much.'

He wasn't so keen on staying now, even if she did offer him something to eat. There was something a little spooky about her, the way she kept calling him Matthew when he'd told her it wasn't his name.

'Would you like something to eat? I was going to make a sandwich.'

The oven was quiet and cold. He was wrong. She hadn't been cooking anything.

'Cheese all right?'

He was hungry. It was a long walk back to town. She might be going that way later. If he hung around she might offer him a lift.

'Well, if it's no trouble. Thanks.'

'No trouble at all.' She sliced some bread with a sharp knife. 'Pickle? Cucumber?'

'No cucumber, thanks.'

'Your room's ready.'

What had she said?

'I'm sorry?'

'I knew you'd come back.'

'Er … is that the time … I didn't realise … actually I ought to get on my way.'

'Though you were so long in coming.'

'I'm sorry … look … I think … were you expecting somebody? Because … I just ran after the fire engine, that's all … maybe you were expecting somebody else…'

'It's been ready for so many years, Matthew. All your things. I updated them every year to match the age you would be. And now you're here, after all this time. Now there won't be any reason to go away again, not ever. We'll be happy, you and Mummy. Just like we were always supposed to be.'

He ran for the door, but she had already locked it. He pulled at the handle, his efforts growing more frantic. She walked across the kitchen towards him, her hand still holding the knife.

'Now, I do hope you're not going to be difficult, Matthew,' she said. 'I hope you won't give Mummy any trouble. I dare say people have brainwashed you and told you lies. But don't worry, it will be all right. Mummy's here to look after you now. She isn't going to lose you again.'

Chapter 17

Prisoner

It was a small attic room with a tiny, unopenable window through which he could see the thatched eaves.

'I'm going to have to put you in here for now,' she said. 'Until I think of what to do. You've been a great disappointment to me, Joseph,' she warned him. 'Very much so, I'm afraid. I had high hopes for you – that you weren't that kind of person and that in time I could have told you all about Matthew and then you could have met him and little by little you could have got to know each other and have even been friends. He doesn't see anyone. Hasn't done for a long time. He gets a little bit lonely. But he can't go out, really. It's too dangerous. You're just like all the rest of them. You want to take him from me.'

'Anna…' he began, then he didn't know how to say it. He felt very cold; his limbs were trembling, but he tried to conceal it from her. His blood was like ice in his veins. Jonah must be here, right here, in this very place – taken prisoner and serving a life sentence.

'What?' she said. She was still holding the shotgun. It was a farmer's gun, the kind you used for shooting vermin, or what farmers said was vermin anyway. 'Well? I have a lot to do, Joseph. If you could please be quick.'

'Anna … people are going to come looking for me…'

'I dare say they are, aren't they? But looking isn't finding. They all came looking for Matthew, but they didn't find him either. I wasn't going to let them take him away from me. They're not going to take him from me ever again.'

Joe looked around the room. The window was too small to escape from. There was a bed, a washbasin, a table with a lamp, a chair with a folded towel on it, and an old-fashioned chamber pot with some dried flowers inside. She saw him looking at it.

'You'll just have to take the flowers out and use it when you need to,' she said. 'Till I decide what to do with you and where you can go. I don't know though, I just don't know…'

He swallowed down the fear and the lump in his throat. She was backing towards the door, still holding the shotgun.

'Anna…' he said, '…it isn't Matthew.'

She looked at him angrily, her eyes narrowing.

'It is,' she said. 'He'd been gone for years, but he came back. I always knew he'd come back.'

'It isn't. It's Jonah.'

'It's Matthew. I knew it straight away when I saw him. There he was, he had come to me, after all this time – come home to me, just like I knew he would. I knew he'd come back, I always did. People come back if you love them enough. They always come back.'

'He's not your son, Anna.'

The barrel of the gun lifted and was pointing directly at him.

'He is so. Don't you ever say that.'

'Matthew is in the churchyard, Anna, under the stone. That's where Matthew is. I know it must have been sad and terrible to lose him, but…'

'You don't know anything,' she hissed. The words came out like the venom of a spitting snake. 'They let him die. They could have saved him but they let him die…'

'I'm sure that isn't true, Anna. I'm sure the doctors tried…'

'Were you there?' she screamed at him. 'Were you there? Answer me!'

He shook his head and looked down at his feet.

'No, I wasn't.'

Maybe he could placate her somehow, and then she would let him go. He stifled his fear and tried to look humble.

'Well then!' She lowered the gun a little. 'Now we're getting at the truth. Because I was there. It was my child, my beautiful little baby, and I should know. He was beautiful, even from the moment he was born…'

'I'm sure he was, Anna, but…'

'His eyes were so blue, right from the very start. They were as blue as the sea…'

'Just because Jonah has blue eyes too…'

'Who is this Jonah? I do not know anyone called Jonah! There is only Matthew. That is the only other person in this house.'

Joe swallowed and tried to control his voice, wanting to keep the fear out of it.

'Where is he, Anna?'

'He's safe. Nice and safe. Don't you worry. No one's going to harm him, not this time. No one's going to take him away.'

She seemed to have dropped her guard a little. Joe calculated the distance between him and the door. He wondered if he would make it, how fast he could go, whether he'd get past her and out of the room and, even if he did, how far he would get after that. He might make it downstairs, but then what? The exterior doors would be locked; the keys might not even be in them. She might have taken them out and put them in her pocket or hidden them somewhere.

All the same, maybe it was worth a try. Maybe if he got past her fast enough he could slam the door behind him and lock her inside. Maybe.

She seemed to know what he was thinking and levelled the gun.

'Don't make me do anything I don't want to do, Joseph,' she warned him. 'I don't want to have to hurt anyone. I'm not that kind of person. Not like some.'

His speech came out clear and cold this time, confronting her with the undeniable truth of what kind of a person she was. He surprised himself with his own sudden confidence, barely recognising his own voice.

'You kidnapped him, Anna. Everyone was looking for him ... and you knew where he was. It was evil what you did. It's been two *years* ... and you've kept him, just like ... like an animal!'

She moistened dry lips with her tongue.

'I'm protecting him,' she said. 'You wouldn't understand.'

'You said they let him die, Anna ... that the doctors let Matthew die. So how can he be here now?'

She smiled a beatific, tender smile.

'He came back to me of course, Joseph. Just as I always knew he would. They tried to take him away from me ... they let him go ... when they could have saved him. He was the most beautiful baby, the best of them all ... none of the others had such blue, blue eyes ... and they neglected him and let him go ... and then ... then they told me that I couldn't have any more. No more babies, not ever. But that didn't worry me because I knew that he would come back to me. He promised me he would. And he's a good boy, who keeps his word.'

She suddenly grew girlish, flirtatious even, confidential.

'He's come back before, you know,' she said. 'This isn't the first time.'

'I'm sorry?'

Joe didn't know what else to do, other than to pretend that he hadn't heard her properly.

'First it was a few months later. I saw him.'

'You saw him?'

'Oh yes. I had to go to the city, to sort out some money, about the mortgage and things … I came out of the bank and there he was.'

'But where, Anna? I mean … how?'

'He was just lying there, in his pram.'

'Lying there?'

'And I looked down and saw him, and there he was, with his blue eyes and fair hair, and I could tell he knew who I was, and he was reaching up for me, so I went to take him out of his pram and to bring him home, and I had him in my arms when this woman…' Her voice grew venomous again. '…this woman, this person who had stolen my baby, began to scream and shout and cause a big fuss, and all these people in uniforms came and … oh my, oh my … they just couldn't see … that he was mine … and so … so…'

Tears ran down her face. She brushed them away with the back of her hand.

'…so they took him away again. A second time. They took him away.'

The fear Joe felt had momentarily gone. All he felt was pity and sadness. Somebody should have helped her a long time ago. Or maybe they had. Perhaps they had tried and failed – the blow to her mind had been too severe and permanent. Maybe some things could never be put right.

Yet she had seemed so perfectly … well … normal. He'd liked her. He'd looked forward to the tea and the cake and her company, to the way she'd treated him as grown up and responsible and had let him help with the lambs. In contrast to the owners of Mystic Moments, he'd always thought of her as sensible, level-headed and impeccably sane.

She propped the gun against the wall, took a tissue out and blew her nose. He thought of grabbing the shotgun, but he didn't try. He was afraid he wouldn't be fast enough, and he wasn't sure how to use one anyway, or if he could. By the time he had screwed up the courage to risk it, the gun was back in her hands.

'Anyway,' she said, 'that's how it was. Someone else had stolen him. Some other woman had taken my child. And nobody would do anything to remedy the injustice! Can you believe that!'

Her anger and indignation lasted only a few seconds, then dissolved into tenderness.

'But he still came back to me, just like I knew he would. And there he was again,' she smiled. 'It took a while, but there he was. Three years old and growing, and there he was, in the park, in his pushchair. But do you know…'

The dark storm clouds gathered again.

'When I tried to take him and bring him home … the whole thing started again … the whole … hysteria … these … this woman … saying he was hers when he was mine all the time and … well … what could I do? What can you do when they're all in league against you – the authorities there and everyone in uniform. So I just had to hurry away … for Matthew's sake … but I knew … I knew that one day, when he was older, when he was big enough to get away, he would come to me. I began to get his room ready. So it would be there waiting for him when he came, and he'd be safe there, and no one could find him and take him back. It was a long, long wait, Joseph. Sometimes I feared he had forgotten me, that he wasn't coming after all, that something bad had happened. Because there are bad people out there, some very bad, evil people, you know, who'll do anything to other people's children. But then there he was. After all the unhappiness, all the years and tears and … there he was. He'd come to me. Asking his mother if he could have a glass of water. Well, of course he could. What loving mother would begrudge her child a glass of water?'

'But, Anna…'

She wasn't listening.

'But you know what they'd done to him?' she said. 'They'd made him think he wasn't Matthew at all. They'd told him all kinds of lies. They'd not even told him about me – not even said that I was his mother.'

'Anna…'

'We had to work on that,' she said. 'It took a while for him to understand that he was Matthew.' Then she brightened up. 'But we're over that hurdle now. He knows who he is. There's no problem with that any more.'

'Anna…'

'I remembered all his birthdays too,' she said brightly. 'And I updated everything every year in his room. Because, after all, he'd be growing up, he'd be getting older. He wouldn't be wanting paints and crayons and childish things when he was growing older. He'd want a computer and some computer games and all the things that boys like to have. So I updated everything, every year, thinking that, well, if he comes now, he won't be disappointed, he'll have all the things he needs.'

'Anna…'

But what was he going to say? Anna, you need help? Anna, you need counselling? Anna, you need a good long holiday? Anna, you're a freak? Anna, you need a straitjacket and a padded room? Anna, you need some kind of medication? Anna, you need love and sympathy and someone to care for you? What do you say to someone so unbalanced and devastated by grief that they would do a thing like this?

'So now he's here.' She smiled. 'Now he's here. And then you came by and I thought that maybe once we got to know each other I might be able to trust you and he could have a friend … but no … no, I was wrong about that. Because you're like all the rest, Joseph. You want to take him from me too.'

'I don't,' he said. 'It's not that…'

'It is,' she said. 'It's that exactly.'

Which they both knew to be true.

'Anna … where is he?'

'He's safe.'

'Where? Is he here?'

'Of course he's here. He's where he wants to be, with his mother.'

Joe suppressed a shudder. There was something horrific about her calmness and conviction. He felt nauseous; he willed it to pass. He tried to look pleasant and to keep his voice level.

'Is it a nice room you had ready for him?'

'It's the best … it's a real boy's room … the right colours and wallpaper. And he's safe in there. No one can get in.'

You mean no one can get out, don't you, Anna? That's what you really mean. He's a prisoner, locked away.

'Can I see him?'

She looked at him, undecided.

'I'll think about that,' she said. 'But I'm not promising anything. Maybe, if he wants, I'll take you down.'

It was in the cellar then, down in the basement, behind thick walls, under quiet earth. If you called, no one would hear you. Maybe he was too afraid to call. Maybe he had done so once and lived to regret it.

'He's got a television,' she added, almost with a sense of pride. 'And I get him videos and DVDs. He's up to date with everything. And we don't neglect his studies either. I get the curriculum papers and the necessary books. He won't get to sit the exams of course, but exams aren't everything. Exams are just marks and points. Real knowledge goes deeper than that, I always say.'

'What if something happens to you, Anna? Who'd look after him then?'

She shrugged off the idea.

'I'm always careful,' she said. 'I'm a good mother.'

'I'm sure you are, Anna.'

'Better than yours,' she said spitefully, 'letting her son go riding off on his own, not knowing or caring where he's going or who he's talking to.'

'That's not true!'

'The truth hurts, huh?'

'Giving somebody freedom isn't neglect.'

'You don't say so? Well, let me tell you, it's not my idea of responsible parenthood!'

He almost burst out laughing. He was having a conversation about responsible parenting with a woman who had abducted a child and held him prisoner for two whole, intolerable years.

'What's so funny? What's to smile at?'

He said nothing.

'Well, I'm going to go now. I have to decide what to do. I'm going to lock the door, and don't try to open it. You won't be able to anyway, but if I hear you try I'll have to come up here and I don't know what I'll do but I'll have to do something to make you stop – and I really don't want to do that. So it'll be best if you don't put me in that situation and make me do something I'd rather not. Understand?'

'Yes. I understand.'

'Good. I'll bring you something to eat in a while.'

'I'm not hungry.'

'You will be. You'll get hungry.'

She slipped out through the door. He heard her turning the key in the lock. It was a double lock and he heard it go round twice. It was a mortise lock too, set into the wood. She was right – even if he tried he wouldn't be able to break it. She'd hear him long before he got through.

He heard the sound of her footsteps recede, the old, warped and bent wood of the staircase creaking under her. He looked around the room – there wasn't a straight line in it. Everything had been twisted with time. Under other circumstances the room would have had a certain kind of olde-worlde charm, but as things were it was a prison cell, despite its floral-patterned wallpaper and gingham curtains.

Joe moved the chair and stood on it so he could see out of the small window. It wasn't a great view. He could just make out the yard below and an adjacent field and the thatch of the roof above.

He got down and sat on the bed, wondering what to do and what she would do, and how long it would be before anyone came to look for him.

Chapter 18

Night

It wouldn't be long, surely. His mother would come home from the shop and when he wasn't there she would give him half an hour or so, thinking that perhaps he had had a puncture or had decided to take a detour that day. Or perhaps, as the weather was fine, he might have fallen asleep in a field.

Then when he still didn't return, she would ring him. His phone!

Anna hadn't thought of that – she hadn't searched him or anything. He still had his phone.

No he didn't. He had dropped it, out in the yard.

He climbed back up on to the chair again, looking down into the patch of the yard that was visible, wondering if he could see the phone.

He couldn't, but he heard it faintly. It was playing his tune, the one he'd made up and programmed into it. The tune repeated, over and over. Anna must have heard it too, for she appeared in the yard with something in her hand made of metal – a hammer or a crowbar, he couldn't quite make out which.

The phone fell silent and she carefully picked up the pieces so that there would be nothing to find, then she carried them off somewhere out of sight. A short while afterwards he heard the door again as she came back into the kitchen.

How long before somebody came? An hour? A few hours? A couple of days? A week? Surely not as long as that?

They must have come before too, when Jonah went missing. Eventually they must have spread the net this wide, even if in doing so they spread it too thinly. They probably didn't even search the place, just made a few informal enquiries – had she heard or seen anything or noticed anything strange? No, she hadn't? Well, thank you all the same, ma'am, and don't forget, if you do remember anything...

She'd have nodded and commiserated and looked concerned. A boy gone missing, that was terrible, terrible. Only it wasn't a boy gone missing for her, it was a son found, the wanderer returned, the lost lamb come back to the fold.

How long?

Wouldn't be today. Possible, but unlikely. They'd start the search nearer to home. Or would they? Did his mother know the routes he took? Not really, not with any precision. He didn't think he'd ever described them to her, and even if he had she wouldn't have paid much attention, or not enough to remember them.

Maybe somebody had seen him. Somebody *must* have seen him, at least in the early part of the journey.

But then people had seen Jonah too. He still vanished, and nobody saw that happen. It was like a conjuror's sleight of hand. Now you see him, now you don't – the Amazing Disappearing Boy.

No, they wouldn't come tonight. Tonight they might start to make enquiries. First they'd ask if he could have run away, if there had been any trouble at home – which his mother would indignantly deny. Then after a while they'd begin to search locally, then to make wider, more general enquiries.

Then, if they had any sense, which they surely did, they'd link the two disappearances, his and Jonah's, and they'd open the old files and start looking all over the county.

Maybe tomorrow then. Tomorrow morning. Tomorrow night at the very latest, most pessimistic estimate.

What would they do when they came? Would they search the place?

No.

They wouldn't suspect her. Why should they? She was a woman, pleasant and friendly and willing to help. She wasn't the kind of stranger they warned you against. No, they wouldn't search the place at all, just take a look in the barn and outbuildings...

'If that's OK with you, ma'am.'

'Yes, of course. Go ahead.'

Obliging, willing to help, nothing to hide.

What if he or Jonah made a noise?

Jonah either wouldn't or couldn't or, even if he did, the cellar room must be so soundproofed and insulated that nobody would hear him anyway.

He wondered about Jonah's state of mind. Two years in this place, with this woman, confined to one room.

I wonder, Joe thought, if he's gone mad yet?

Had it been him, he felt sure he would have done. But maybe Jonah had more resilience.

They were so near to each other too, separated by only a few metres of stone and earth. That was all. Jonah was just a short distance away.

'Jonah! Jonah! It's me! Joe!'

So near but so far. He called Jonah's name, again and again, until his throat was raw, but it was useless.

An hour passed. There was a sound at the door. She unlocked and opened it and brought in some food, holding a tray in one hand and the gun in the other.

'Here,' she said. 'No reason to go hungry.'

As she put down the tray, he wondered if he could make it to the door. But he was still sure that he would get no further than the bottom of the stairs. As she was going he murmured, 'Thanks.' Not that he was grateful, he just didn't want to get on the wrong side of her.

'I'm still thinking what to do with you,' she warned him as she left. 'Don't force me into any quick decisions, because quick decisions won't be good ones … not for you. And I heard you shouting. Don't do it again or I'll gag you. There's no one here called Jonah anyway.'

Then the door closed and she was locking it again.

She'd been thinking the exact same thoughts as his own, he knew it. She'd been sitting down there in the kitchen, running the same things through her mind. How long before he was missed, how long before anyone came, what to do when they did?

What was she going to do with him?

Put it another way, what *could* she do with him? If he were her, what would *he* do with him?

He'd make him vanish, that's what he would do. He'd have no choice, absolutely no alternative. He wouldn't keep two people prisoner, not indefinitely, not like that.

If he were her, he'd kill him.

If he was going to be calm, cool, detached and logical about it, and not let emotions bother him or anything like that, then he'd kill him.

What else was there to do?

Let him go? Impossible. Keep him there? For how long? For days, weeks, years, until he grew large enough to tower above her? He and Jonah together could easily overpower her…

He heard the outer door slam downstairs, then he heard what he thought was her locking it from the outside. He stood on the chair and peered out of the window. He saw her crossing the yard, carrying a bag of feed.

She was off to tend the animals.

He almost laughed. Here she was, mad, unhinged, with a prisoner in the cellar and another in the attic room, and she was off to care for her animals. In fact, she'd said as much to him once when they'd been sitting in the kitchen with tea and slices of cake, he remembered.

'I hate cruelty to animals, you know. I simply don't know how anybody could let a poor, dumb animal suffer.'

Ha! Poor, dumb animals maybe, but the not so poor, not so dumb kind … her compassion didn't seem to extend that far. In fact they could be kept locked up for as long as she pleased.

He lost sight of her. He got down from the chair and looked at the tray she had brought. There was a can of Coke on it, a slice of cake, an apple and a sandwich.

He drank the Coke. He couldn't eat. After drinking, he needed to use the toilet. Instead of using the chamber pot, he went to the sink, turned both the taps on and used the sink instead. He let the taps run for a good while after, so that everything was washed away. He washed his hands – the hot water was almost scalding.

He looked at the bottles on the small glass shelf above the sink – hand creams and lotions, a tube of toothpaste, caked with paste like dried cement around the nozzle, and an old bottle of perfume. He unscrewed the stopper and smelt it. He poured a little of it into the sink, then ran the taps again.

Outside, the sky was changing, night was beginning to fall. His mother would be wondering where he was. She might ring Frea first before she rang anybody else, asking her what to do. She was like that – diffident, wanting someone else to take a lead so that she could follow.

What would Frea say? She'd ask Ran. But what good was being a Druid and all the rest when someone had disappeared and not come home?

He'd tell her to go to the police. It all came down to that in the end. It didn't matter how way-out you were, when things went wrong you still turned to the people you wanted nothing to do with most of the time and didn't have a good word for.

A light came on in the yard. He could hear the sheep bleating and baaing. A horse whinnied. She must be in the stables now, taking care of them.

Then she came back into the house. There were vague sounds for a time coming from downstairs. Perhaps she was cooking, making herself a meal. He couldn't smell anything though. Maybe she was just warming up some soup, or cutting herself a sandwich like the one she had made him.

What about Jonah? When did he eat?

The house fell silent as darkness enclosed it. The night-time noises of the countryside sounded intermittently – birds, small animals, creatures of the dark.

He heard a voice. It was her. Out in the yard again. She was talking to somebody. Maybe it was the police. Maybe they had already come. He just needed to make a noise then, to smash something, to break the small window, shatter the glass. They'd hear, they'd come running into the house, their feet pounding on the stairs, their shoulders at the door, and then he'd be out, he'd be…

It wasn't the police.

He stood up on the chair, on tiptoe, straining to see as much as he could.

It was a boy. His feet were shackled with something that looked like old slave chains, like the ones he had seen in books. But it couldn't have been that, it must have been some ancient farm fetters for restraining animals and beasts.

'Isn't it a lovely night, Matthew?' she was saying. 'So cool and clear…'

The figure shuffled around, unable to go far or to move much other than to hobble around the yard.

Fresh air and exercise. So that was it. Every night perhaps, in the silence and darkness, in the yard of the small farm. There were few enough passers-by in the day – at night there was no one at all.

He strained to see Jonah's face but was unable to. He had grown though, was taller, had filled out. His fair hair looked silver in the light of the moon. It was him, and yet it wasn't the Jonah he had known; time had separated them – the two years were between them like an expanse of desert.

'Jonah … Jonah!'

It came out as a whisper. Pathetically, he waved, though he couldn't be seen and he knew it. Then he filled his lungs and shouted.

'Jonah! Jonah! It's me!'

The words flew into the night like startled birds. Anna looked up angrily towards the window, but Jonah didn't seem to have heard. He went on dragging the chains, shuffling round and round.

'Isn't it a lovely night, Matthew,' Joe heard Anna say again after a while. 'Such a lovely star-filled night?'

Jonah didn't answer her. He walked in silence around the yard as she kept up a burble of inconsequential conversation. Or rather it was more of a monologue, for all the time that she went on talking he didn't say a word. Finally she announced that: 'I guess it's time to go back in.'

Joe didn't call out his name again. In truth, he was afraid of what Anna might do to him. It didn't do to anger the jailer when you were at the jailer's mercy.

The shuffling figure followed her, out of Joe's field of vision. Then both of them were gone and the yard was empty and silent again, apart from the cry of an owl and the whinnying horses settling down for the night.

Joe felt a tingle of horror at the spectacle he had just seen, at the awful, somehow mundane ordinariness of it. It was a scene that must have been repeated over and over until it had become quite natural to its two participants – the set routine of a certain hour. It was a nightly ritual to them – something you did, like brushing your teeth before bedtime.

He got off the chair and sat on the bed. He had never understood before how anything could be said to make your flesh creep. How could it creep? It was impossible, a total exaggeration. But now he knew. It was like insects all over his body.

The world was silent again. They weren't coming – no police, no searchers. Not tonight. Tomorrow maybe, or the day after. He lay down on the bed without undressing, and he slept.

But they didn't come the next day either. In the morning Anna brought him some breakfast. She also brought him a toothbrush. She was taciturn and refused to answer his questions or reveal any of her plans – or if she had even formulated any.

The day dragged interminably. When she brought him food again he asked for something to read. She returned with some books, and when she did, he asked to use the proper toilet. She refused and told him to use the chamber pot, then she locked him in once more. But he hadn't really wanted to use it – he'd just wanted to see what she would do.

The books she had brought him were recently published ones, no more than a year old; they must have come from Jonah's room. Had she given Jonah a reason for taking them? Had she told him that there was someone else in the house?

Joe resolved to shout to him again tonight, no matter what Anna did afterwards. He'd wait until she brought

Jonah out into the yard and then he'd yell his name at the top of his voice and tell him that it was Joe and that someone would be coming and not to give up now – there was hope.

Only she didn't bring Jonah out. There was no exercise that night. Perhaps she had anticipated Joe's intentions and taken pre-emptive action. Joe forced himself to stay awake, but they didn't appear.

However, the police might. Maybe that was the reason. He'd been missing nearly two days now. His mum would have told them about his bike rides. They'd be widening the radius of the search – wouldn't they?

It was long after midnight. His eyes were heavy. Yet what if he slept and they came and he missed them? All the same, he did feel dog-tired now, drained and exhausted by the shock and fear of all that had happened. He ate some of the cold food from his tray, then he lay on the bed and closed his eyes.

He slept a few hours. It was maybe two or three in the morning when he woke again, panicked and afraid, woken by sudden noise and light and the distant sound of a dog barking. The door was thrown open and she burst in.

'They're coming,' she said. 'Don't you dare say anything. Don't you say a thing!'

But she wasn't really giving him the chance. In her hand was tape and rope and before he had even properly woken his mouth was sealed and his hands and ankles were bound to the bedposts.

'Don't you make a sound!' she whispered. She put her finger to her lips. As if he had any choice in the matter.

She locked the door and went back down the stairs.

Shortly afterwards he heard the car arrive. He could make out the blue, revolving light, reflected on the ceiling. Then there was a knock at the door, the sound of locks and bolts, and Anna's voice, pretending to be tired and bleary-eyed.

'Good evening, ma'am.'

'What is it? Whatever is the matter?'

'We're sorry to disturb you, ma'am, at this hour of day…'

'It's the middle of the night. I was just going to get some sleep. I've been up with one of the lambs … I was just up in the attic room, fetching some medicine … you maybe saw the light…'

'We're sorry to disturb you, ma'am, it's just that we're looking for somebody. It's quite serious…'

'Oh…'

'Could we come in for a moment?'

'Of course.'

Into the kitchen. Maybe she would even put the kettle on, offer them tea.

How could he make a noise? Maybe if he squirmed around he could break the knots holding him and then roll right off the bed. They'd be sure to hear him when he crashed on to the floor. They'd look up, puzzled.

'What was that, ma'am?'

'Oh, just the water pipes … the pigeons … a squirrel in the loft … a mousetrap going off…'

'If you don't mind, ma'am, we'll just take a little look up there, if we may…'

If he could just get off the bed.

He struggled and squirmed, but he couldn't. The knots bit into him and seemed to get tighter. His feet felt numb, his wrists burned.

He tried to bounce on the mattress. Maybe the springs would squeak.

Barely a sound. Useless. He was tied too tight.

If he could knock something over then – the table lamp maybe, or the chamber pot with the flowers in it sitting on the dresser. Maybe he could do it with the power of his mind. If looks could kill ... then they ought to be able to shift old chamber pots.

Only looks didn't kill. It was people who did that, with fingers on triggers. It was guns and knives that killed, and looks were no defence against them.

He could hear them going.

They couldn't be, not already. They'd only been there ten minutes. What about the outbuildings? What about the barn? Weren't they going to look in there? Were they just going to take her word for it?

If they searched they might find his bike. She wouldn't have left it where it was. It might be in the barn, behind some bales. Or was it also at the bottom of the big pile of compost?

Jonah.

Jonah, make a sound. From the room down there, from your prison cell. Call or scream or yell or anything. The time of captivity and rage. Let it all come out in one great immense scream, quick, Jonah, before they go.

Do it now!

Please!

Maybe he was too cowed and afraid. Maybe he called but no one heard. Perhaps he too was bound and gagged. Or simply fast asleep.

So nothing. Silence. Then voices out in the yard. The creak of the barn doors opening and the sounds of the outbuildings being searched. She'd be putting the lights on and offering to get torches, for those dark, inaccessible corners – though they had their own flashlights, of course, but it looked good to be obliging.

They'd kick the straw up and peer behind the bales; she'd help them look, and then lead them to the stables, calming the horses as they searched around in there, knowing full well that there was nothing to find. It was all in the cottage, encased in silence, like a body in concrete.

What *had* she done with his bike then? Joe wondered. Maybe it was in the back of the Land Rover. Or down in the basement. Or already dismantled and lying in pieces under the green slime of a drainage ditch.

'Well, thank you for your time, Ms Starne.'

'No trouble at all, officer.'

'And if you do hear or see anything?'

'I'll be in touch immediately.'

'Thank you.'

'Well, good luck, I hope he turns up soon.'

'We hope so too.'

An engine fired into life. The blue, intermittent light came on. Then someone must have thought there was no need for it and turned it off.

Now, Jonah. It's your last chance. Scream! Now!

The car drove away. The engine sound became distant. The silence and the night re-entered, like two actors claiming the stage. The other players had played their parts, said their lines and gone.

Joe lay there, a cold sweat on his forehead, filled with hopelessness and defeat. After a while he remembered that his limbs and joints were aching. The pain cut through his despair and he wondered when she would come to untie the bonds.

He heard her coming up the stairs, then going into the bathroom. He waited, tense, for her to finish, to walk up the next flight and enter his room.

But she didn't. She went to her own bedroom and closed the door. She had forgotten all about him and would leave him there until morning.

He realised that the police hadn't even suspected her. She'd been so convincing, so transparently honest and decent, that they'd taken her word for everything. They'd have been anxious not to waste any more time here and to move on to the next call on the list.

178

But perhaps they'd still come back – something would occur to one of them, some inconsistency, something suspicious. Joe listened hard for the return of the police car. It didn't come.

Eventually, despite his discomfort, he fell asleep, to be woken a few hours later by the numbness in his legs and arms.

He hoped she would remember him soon. He hoped she wouldn't leave him like this forever.

Chapter 19

Day

In the morning he heard the radio go on, somewhere down in the house. It wasn't music, but people talking. She probably had it tuned to the news. He guessed that he might be on it, but the thought didn't console him. The police weren't going to come back, at least not for a long time. Why should they? If they had felt any real suspicion about the place they would have taken it apart before they left.

She was out on the landing, unlocking the door. She came in with a tray with some breakfast on it. She put the tray down on the dresser, then she came over and released him. She didn't apologise for having left him like that all night.

'Well then…'

She looked at him as he sat trying to massage some life back into his feet and wrists. Her face was different now and he wondered why he had ever thought she was pretty. She looked hard and mean this morning, full of anger and resentment.

'You had to go and find that rucksack, didn't you?' she said – as if the fault was all his for unearthing the truth, and not hers for burying it. 'You couldn't leave well alone. You had to stick your nose in where it wasn't wanted. Well, you know what curiosity did, don't you?'

He knew all right. It had killed the cat. Joe tried to sit up. For the moment, standing was out of the question.

'What about his sweatshirt?' he asked, suddenly remembering. 'They found it, didn't they, hundreds of miles away. How did that get there?'

She gave a tight, crafty smile.

'How do you think?' she said.

'But why?' he asked.

She looked at him, not understanding.

'Why? I didn't think you were stupid, Joseph. To stop them looking, of course. To put them off the scent.'

'Yes, but why do that?' he said. 'If it's Matthew and he's yours, why hide him away and lock him up and keep him like a prisoner? Why take his clothes hundreds of miles away and leave them somewhere where you know they'll be found, so that everyone will think that was where he'd been taken…'

She folded her arms.

What did that mean?

Joe tried to remember. He had read a book about body language once. When people stood like that and folded their arms tightly, it meant that they were putting a wall up, didn't it, between themselves and the rest of the world? They were protecting themselves against unpleasant truths.

'They took him away once,' she said. 'If they could, they'd take him away again. Only they're not going to. We've got each other now and it's going to stay that way. We don't need anyone or anybody else…'

She studied him a moment, still hiding behind the barrier of her folded arms.

'And that,' she told him, 'includes you.'

Joe swallowed. He had managed to sit up on the edge of the bed. He didn't try to stand. If he did, he knew his ankles wouldn't take his weight and he'd fall over. She brought the tray over and placed it on the bed next to him.

'There,' she said.

She turned to go.

'Anna…'

She stopped but didn't speak, then she grew impatient. It was the only card he had and he was hesitant to play it, because if he did and he didn't win the trick…

'Well? What?'

'What about *my* mother?'

'*Your* mother?'

'Yes. You lost your son … she's lost me now … she's at home, sick with worry, wondering where I am.'

'I got my son back,' she said. 'He's here with me now.'

'But you know what it's like,' Joe said. 'When you first lost him, you didn't know then that he would come back, did you? You must have thought that you had lost him forever … that's how my mother must feel now.'

She nodded.

'Well, I'm very sorry about that,' she said. 'And I wouldn't put another mother through a thing like that if I had any choice about it. But I don't.'

'Yes, but…'

'I don't have a choice because of your spying and nosing and looking in places that don't concern you and finding things that have nothing to do with you. If you'd been a good son and had had a moment's consideration for your own mother you would have stayed at home with her and never brought all this trouble on her.'

'But Anna…'

'It's your doing. I feel sorry for that poor woman, yes I do. But that's because she has a bad son. Thankfully my own son is not like that and he stays at home and looks after me and I look after him, and he doesn't go gallivanting all over the country, putting his nose into other people's business when he ought to be at home with his mother!'

'You asked me here. You asked me in.'

'I thought you had possibilities as a friend for my Matthew. But now I see that you're the wrong sort of boy, Joseph. Just look at the grief you've brought to your mother. Yes, like it or not, that's the sort of boy you are.'

He saw it was quite impossible to argue with her, to have even the most basic of rational discussions. It was his fault or, if not his, someone else's. It would never be hers. It was the hospital's fault, the midwife's fault, the doctor's fault – when in reality it was probably nobody's fault at all. They had probably done everything they could to save her son. Maybe he had been premature, born too small and too soon to survive.

Joe wondered about the father, what had happened to him, where he had gone.

'Anna…'

She turned in the doorway.

'What's going to happen to me?'

'I'm still thinking,' she said. 'But I don't have many options, as far as I can see.'

'The options being?' he said, trying to keep the fear out of his voice.

'You'll find out,' she said. 'Once I've decided.'

Then she left, closed the door and locked it behind her.

Later in the morning, he thought he heard a car draw up in the yard. He climbed on to the chair, looked down, and saw the red bonnet of what he presumed was the post van. Anna was out in the yard, driving the tractor. Joe saw the postman cross towards her, some letters in his hand. Joe began to shout and to beat at the attic window. As he did so, the engine of the tractor started to rev, drowning out the sound.

The postman waved to Anna, then disappeared from view. He must have gone to leave the letters in the porch. Maybe he thought it odd that she hadn't got down from the tractor, or maybe he was used to that – farmers were busy people, they didn't always stop for a chat and a word about the weather.

The engine roared louder and louder, as if she was testing it out, listening for the recurrence of some trouble.

The postman reappeared, the door of the van opened and closed, then he drove away.

He hadn't heard a sound.

The tractor went quiet. Then there was another noise. It was her, coming up the stairs, running up, two, three steps at a time. She could hardly unlock the door fast enough. Then she burst in, the shotgun in her hands, her face pale with anger.

'Don't you ever do that again!' she hissed, all but sticking the barrel of the gun into his face. 'You want me to gag you and truss you up all the time? Is that what you want?'

He stood, his back to the wall, too terrified to speak.

'Well, do you! Do you?'

He shook his head.

'Then don't make a sound! Matty and I, we don't like it! Now then!'

She lowered the gun.

'There won't be anyone else coming now anyway. But you make another sound and I'll tie you up and forget you're up here and you can just lie here for days and days!'

She backed out of the room and slammed the door. He heard her lock it again.

'Not a sound!' she called through the door, as she went back down the stairs.

The long morning passed, minute by heavy minute. He listened for any and every sound – a car on the road, a siren, for the police returning, for some clever officer to realise something had not been right about the place, about the woman, about her story...

No one's coming, his worst thoughts told him. They're all out looking but they're not coming here. They're searching every inch of land, the fields near the town, the hedgerows, the ditches, the irrigation channels, under the willows and the cypress trees ... but they're not coming here again.

They're opening up the old files, looking at similar cases, going through all the notes and facts of Jonah's disappearance. They're looking at the names of any men with records and histories, and they're going round to find them and check up on what they've been doing and where they've been doing it. They're maybe even taking suspects' belongings away in sealed bags to look for fibres and DNA – *my* DNA.

But they're not coming here. They're not coming here because she's pretty in her way – even if she doesn't look it to me any longer – and because she's a woman, on her own, trying to make ends meet and keep the place going and hold it all together somehow, and you have to admire that, you really do.

She just isn't the kind of person who would do a thing like that. She wouldn't fit the profile. She's above suspicion in every way.

Yet all it would take would be curiosity. Some junior officer, maybe, young and interested and not jaded by time and experience. Or a woman officer – a woman would perhaps be more likely to make the connection. All it needed was for someone to check the records of people in the locality – births and marriages, divorces and deaths.

They'd find it, right there. The stone was in the graveyard, so the baby's death had to be registered. If someone spotted that, they'd know that Matthew Starne's age, had he lived, would now be the same as mine and Jonah's too – the boy who had also vanished, two years ago.

Then a crack would appear, a moment of illumination, like sunlight breaking through cloud. They'd put two and two together and what could they make but four?

Yes, maybe there was somebody doing that, while all the others were out searching the lay-bys and the lanes. Maybe one young, bright, perceptive officer was sitting in front of a computer screen and asking all the right questions.

But Joe knew that nobody was.

They would go on searching until they had to admit that there was no hope of finding him. And all the while he, Jonah and Anna were there, just waiting to be found. But no one would think of looking, and nobody would find them.

He curled up on the bed, rested his head on his arms, and began to cry.

He remembered what she had said about making a noise and how angry she had been and how angry she could get.

So he tried to do it quietly.

Maybe she was too busy to eat lunch, but that meant that he didn't either. By early evening he was hungry, afraid and – to his own surprise, considering his situation – bored.

She could have given him a radio, or a small television. He'd read one of the books she had left him, but found it hard to concentrate.

He paced around the room, which only made him hungrier, but it was better than sitting still. At least he had water. He ran the tap, let the water fill his cupped hands and drank, then dried his hands. He picked up the bottle of perfume and sniffed at it. Strange that she would have perfume; she didn't seem like the perfume type – too busy getting her hands dirty and looking after the animals to get dressed up to go out. Maybe once she had known another kind of life.

He heard the noise of the tractor again and stood on the chair to look out of the small window and down into he yard. The machine trundled past, with her in the cab, her hair tied up out of her eyes. It wasn't the tractor though, it was the small digger which he had seen in one of the barns. It was like a toolkit on wheels. Different attachments fitted into it – drilling spikes, ditching scoops, a hedge trimmer, a toothed kind of bucket for clearing and digging out drainage channels.

Why would she be using that? There'd been no heavy rain, no storms – nothing had fallen to block any of the channels nearby.

Unless she was digging something else – a small, narrow trench maybe, out in one of the fields. Small, narrow and deep. You could throw something down into a trench like that, cover it back over, scatter a handful of seed upon the earth, and nobody would know.

The digger went out of sight. He stood on tiptoe and craned his neck, but could see it no longer. He saw something else though – a field of gold in the far distance, ripening oilseed flowers, yellow as buttercups, a streak of colour in the grey afternoon.

Then he heard the whine of the hydraulics as the scoop of the digger bit down into the earth, chewed up a large chunk, spat it out and went for another. The whine continued, intermittently, for half an hour, then it stopped and the engine fell silent.

He heard her out in the yard again, calling to one of the cats, making a fuss of it probably, tickling its chin and behind its ears, asking if it had caught any mice. Then he heard the door as she entered the kitchen.

She must have fed Jonah first, then the cats, then herself. Finally she brought some food up for him, something hot.

'There. That's yours.'

'Anna…'

She was already at the door, on her way out. She didn't seem to like him using her name now. It made him too human.

'Well?'

'Have you decided?'

She didn't answer immediately.

'I'm still thinking about it.'

He knew then that she *had* decided, and he knew what her decision was. It was the only decision she could make. She couldn't keep both of them. Two prisoners – that was impossible. One of them would have to go. As soon as it could be done. And the one to go wouldn't be 'Matthew'.

She'd been out in the field, digging his grave for him. She'd do it tonight.

Nobody would notice. If they heard, they wouldn't even be curious. They'd just think it was somebody out after rabbits, or a farmer shooting that pest of a fox, which had got into the hen house again.

Night was falling. The food grew cold on the tray where she had left it. Darkness came.

There was no way out. Was there? The window was too high and too small. He couldn't break down the door, and even if he did, how far would he get? What escape was there? Who'd ever hear a cry for help?

Then a thought came to him. They didn't have to hear. They only had to see. And there was a way to do it – something they would see from miles away, as far away as the distant Tor with the ruined tower upon it, as far away as the town.

It was what – indirectly – had brought him here, and Jonah too. In its way it was responsible for everything. There was one cry he could give that everyone would notice.

Fire.

Chapter 20

Fire

At first Jonah had believed that she was going to let him go, that it was all some kind of bizarre joke. Then he saw how serious she was and how truly she believed that he was who she said he was. When he disagreed with that, she became upset – worse than upset: unpleasant, vengeful, spiteful. She withheld food, she left him in the dark, day after day, not even letting him out at night to shuffle around the yard.

'We all have to learn,' she'd say. 'Children have to learn and boys are especially difficult, as we all know. Tough love, it's called, Matthew. I don't want to be cruel, but if it means being kind in the end, then that's what we'll have to do. Now then, Matthew...'

'My name isn't Matthew.'

'You're being stubborn again, Matthew, stubborn and wilful and you're not being nice to Mummy after all Mummy's done for you.'

'You're not my mother and my name isn't Matthew.'

'Well, I'm just going to have to leave you in the dark again then, Matthew. Not because I want to, but because I'm afraid you've picked up some very bad habits since you've been away. You've been with the wrong kind of people and I'm afraid you just have to be cured of that one way or another, even if tough love is what it takes. You hear me, Matthew?'

'My name isn't Matthew and you'd better let me go or somebody's going to come for me and you'll be in such big trouble...'

'I'm afraid I'm going to have to take the light bulb with me now, Matthew, and to lock the door. You're going to have to be on your own in the dark again until you learn your lesson. I'm not saying there are rats down here, but maybe you ought to think about that and be grateful that you don't have the kind of mother who would leave you alone in the dark with rats. I don't want to do this, Matthew, but you're making me, do you hear? You're treating your mother very badly. You're not a loving son. When I have the farm to look after too. All right, Matthew? So you know why I'm doing this? It isn't to hurt you; it's for your own good.'

'My name's not Matthew.'

She took a cloth to protect her hand from the heat of the bulb, removed it from the ceiling socket and left the room. The door closed behind her, the bolt slid home, and there was absolute, total darkness.

She didn't come back for twenty-four hours.

After this had happened a few times, it was hard to really know who you were, if you were Matthew or Jonah or any one of a hundred other names. And, in a sense, what did it matter what you were called? One name was as good as another. Everyone was somebody different to other people – everyone saw different aspects of your personality. You were still yourself inside after all, no matter what name you were given.

Prisoners were given numbers, weren't they? They were robbed of their identity as part of their punishment. So it would be a kind of number. A label for the duration of imprisonment. He'd go along with it – anything just to survive.

'Matthew…'

'Yes?'

'Well, that's better, much better … Matthew…'

'Yes?'

'Why don't you call me "Mother" sometimes?'

'You're not my mother.'

'Matthew, you know that's not so. It's wicked and hurtful to say a thing like that. Just when I thought you were improving too, but I see you still have these defects of character. You just don't seem able to learn your lesson. So I'm going to have to leave you in the dark again for a while. I don't want to, but you're making me.'

So it went on. Darkness, no food for a while, the loss of any sense of the passage of time, until at length…

'Matthew…'

'Yes…'

'See what Mummy's brought you? Something nice to eat, and light to see by, and some books and things. What do you say?'

'Thanks.'

'What do you say?'

'Thank you.'

'Thank you who, Matthew?'

'Thanks – Mother.'

'That's much better. Now we can really start to enjoy each other and catch up on all the missing years.'

'Yes – Mother.'

If you say so. As you please. Matthew, Mother, whoever, whatever. What did it matter? Bend with the wind a little, blow with the breeze, even let her think that you're beaten. All that really matters is survival. Just always keep a part of you to yourself, a secret, untouchable part, right down at the core, a part that is always and forever you, which nobody can violate. Otherwise, you just lose yourself, or go mad.

He could tell that for now there was to be no escape. His only refuge was to endure.

Joe thought of Christmas. Vegetarian nut roast usually, with veggie Christmas pudding to follow. His mother didn't drink much, and when she did it was usually white wine, but she always kept a small bottle of brandy in the cupboard for splashing over the pudding. The pudding had to be hot of course – hot enough to make the brandy vaporise. When it began to vaporise, you put a match to it and the top of the Christmas pudding caught fire.

Alcohol was highly inflammable.

Yes, alcohol burned and perfume was alcohol. He'd heard Ran and Frea talking about it in the shop. A customer had come in asking for alcohol-free scent. She'd said that alcohol had bad karma and it affected her spiritual equilibrium. Frea had directed her towards the small bottles of natural oils.

After she'd gone, Ran – always keen to be the expert – had explained to Joe how perfume was made. He'd said that most brand-name perfumes were fragrances preserved in pure, odourless alcohol. He'd even made a joke about getting drunk on aftershave, then had rapidly started back-pedalling, warning Joe against it, afraid he might actually drink some just to see what it was like and make himself sick or go blind.

Joe crossed to the sink, took the three-quarters-full bottle of perfume, unscrewed the top and smelt the contents. It wasn't like the stuff his mother used – not sandalwood or anything like that. It was proper expensive perfume in a designer bottle.

He dabbed some on to the back of his hand. It felt cold. The alcohol vaporised, leaving the essence of the perfume behind it.

He didn't have a match. How to light it then? The bulb?

He tried the table lamp first, but the bulb was dead. So he moved the chair over, stood on it and felt the bulb of the ceiling light with his hand.

'Ow!'

It was scorching hot. He instantly recoiled, nearly falling off the chair. Had she heard him call out? Would she come up? If she came into the room and smelt the perfume, would she work out what he'd been trying to do?

He stood, frozen to the chair. There were sounds from far away in the house. She hadn't heard him. She didn't come.

Paper then. If he could soak some paper. No, there wasn't any. In the drawers, maybe, lining paper? He opened every one. Nothing. The wardrobe then? Nothing there either.

He removed his fleece, pulled off his T-shirt and put the fleece back on. He took the perfume bottle, splashed a third of its contents on to the T-shirt, then took it to the bare light bulb.

He wrapped the T-shirt around the bulb. The heavy, sickly-sweet scent of evaporating perfume filled the room. The T-shirt grew hot, but that was all. The alcohol just vaporised. The bulb wasn't hot enough to ignite it.

He needed a flame, a match.

Rub two pieces of wood together.

What pieces of wood? And anyway, was that actually possible?

A spark?

A spark might do it – ignite the vaporising alcohol. Only where was he going to get a spark from, unless lightning suddenly struck the room?

He lay on the bed, holding the T-shirt near to his nose, taking some comfort from the smell of the perfume. He closed his eyes for a while and dozed. When he woke again the sky was full of starlight. He stood on the chair and looked out of the window at the sky. It was a clear night, you'd be able to see for miles and miles.

She'd come up soon. First she'd take Jonah out to walk around for a while. The police had been and gone, so she'd let him out again, knowing it was safe to do so.

Jonah would shuffle around the yard for his exercise and fresh air. Joe wondered how long it had been since Jonah had last seen proper daylight.

Then she'd take Jonah back inside. She'd allow a while for him to fall asleep, then she'd come up the stairs, open the door and say, 'You gave me no choice, Joseph. I didn't want to do anything like this but you gave me no choice.'

Unless…

The wall-socket. He got down from the chair and knelt to inspect it. He just needed to get the cover off. If only he had a knife.

Then again, perhaps he didn't need to get the cover off at all. The table lamp, that would do it – if it was going to work at all.

He unplugged the lamp from the socket. The lamp base was made from rough, unglazed ceramic, the kind a beginner might make at an evening pottery class.

He wound the wires around his hand and tugged hard, to rip them out of the lamp.

Now he had a plug with two bare wires attached to it.

Do not try this at home, he thought. Unless you really have to of course. Unless you have no alternative.

He'd seen a programme on TV about accidents in the home, on the dangers of DIY and on the perils of bare wires and amateur electrics. There had even been a public service ad – *Never leave a plug lying around the house with bare, exposed wires attached to it. It could start a fire or electrocute a child.*

Thanks, he thought, for the warning. Now was the time to find out what it was worth.

He peeled back the plastic covering from the heads of the wires, using his nails and his teeth, exposing a couple of centimetres of copper. When a decent amount of wire was visible, he twisted the strands around to finish the ends off neatly.

Next he took the plug, ensured that the wall switch was set to off, and inserted the plug into the socket. He set the wires down, carefully dividing them so that the exposed ends were not in contact, or near enough to short out.

Then he turned the switch on. Now the wires were live.

He took his T-shirt again and poured half the remaining perfume over it. He placed the perfume bottle on the floor near the bared wires. Then he stood on the chair and held the T-shirt to the overhead light. The smell of the perfume filled the air again and became sickly, but he let it go on vaporising – just like the brandy on the Christmas pudding. His arms started to ache.

Got to get it just right, Joe.

The brandy won't ignite
If you don't get it right!

Sometimes it didn't either, and Christmas just wasn't the same then, when the pudding didn't go up in flames. Sometimes his mother had to try it a second time.

Only there wasn't going to be a second time, not here. He had one chance, and one only.

Now?

No. A little longer. Too long and the alcohol would be gone; not enough and it wouldn't catch. Had to allow for cooling down too – time taken moving from here to there. It would happen rapidly. There wouldn't be a second to waste.

'Got the matches ready, Joe? I'm bringing it in from the kitchen. Got to be quick now. Got to catch it just in time.'

'Yes, Mum. I'm ready!'

Now?

Now! Go!

GO!

He dropped from the chair, almost dived across the room, threw the T-shirt down, the alcohol still rising from it in a faint mist. Then he grabbed the wires, held them apart over the vapour rising from the cloth, tensed himself…

And touched the wires together.

Ahhh!

The shock hurled him across the room. He banged his head against the wooden bed. The room was plunged into instant darkness as sparks spat from the wires.

Then the darkness was total.

It hadn't worked. Damn it, damn it, damn it. He'd misjudged it. He could hear her already, moving around downstairs, searching for a torch probably, lighting candles. He must have blown the main fuse in the house.

'Do you have any incense?'

'No.'

'Joss sticks? Scented candles?'

'Well, I've got some candles for when the power goes – plain, ordinary ones.'

'That'll have to do.'

Then Anna had fetched a packet of candles from the drawer.

An eternity ago.

She'd be moving around down there, checking all the fuses, wondering why the lights had blown. It shouldn't take her long. Just a matter of throwing the trip switch. Unless she still had the old-fashioned wire fuses down there.

They'd had them once in a house they'd lived in. Joe could remember his dad mending a blown fuse – putting a screwdriver into his finger in the process. It had taken him half an hour to find some fuse wire, then cut it to length, clean out the old fuse, thread the new one through, tighten up the retaining screws and injure himself.

Five, ten minutes at most then, and no injuries for someone like Anna.

Not that it mattered now. It hadn't worked anyway.

Then he saw a glow – a faint, firefly glow.

He crawled over on hands and knees. A solitary spark was smouldering in the cloth of the T-shirt, on the brink of extinction.

He blew, so lightly, so softly. Too hard and he would kill that vital spark of life. Fire and life – so strong and furious, yet so fragile too. So easy to extinguish in their early stages, but so tenacious once they gathered strength…

It spread a little wider, just a fraction, a centimetre or so.

Burn. Please burn.

A tiny flame appeared in the blackening cloth. The vaporising alcohol fed it and the cloth kept it alive. It flickered and grew. The flame became bigger. He could smell the burning cotton.

There was just enough light to see now. He went and got the chamber pot and grabbed the dry flowers. He held them by the stalks and put their heads into the flame.

They caught. He dropped them back into the chamber pot, snatched up the T-shirt and dropped it in with them.

A pot full of fire. By its light he pulled off the pillowslip and, careful not to kill the fire by adding too much too soon, fed it in.

Soon it was burning. Any moment it would turn to a blaze. Quickly he dragged the chair over to the wardrobe, then he took the pot full of fire and shoved it up on top of the wardrobe. The burning dried flowers almost fell out and ignited his hair; sparks ran over his shoulders.

Get off, get off!

He extinguished the sparks with his hands, beating them out and burning his fingers.

Smoke began to fill the room. The flames were licking the ceiling. Above it were the roof timbers…

And the thatched roof. Bone dry. It hadn't rained in weeks. Dry as tinder.

Once the thatch caught, it would go up like a petrol station.

He pulled the sheet from the bed, took it to the sink and turned on the tap. The basin soon overflowed, but it didn't matter. He soaked the sheet thoroughly. Once it was waterlogged he dragged the wet sheet over towards the door, put it to his mouth and waited. He realised that he had left the plug in the basin and the tap running, but he didn't go back.

He looked up. The fire on top of the wardrobe was starting to ignite the ceiling. It was years old – old and dry. It began to burn and the fire spread up into it, as if consuming dry paper.

The light came back on. One way or another, she'd fixed the fuse.

He crouched down by the door, the fumes filling the room from the ceiling downwards, the bulb dim behind the smoke.

She had to come soon. He'd relied on her coming. Or how else was he to get out? She *had* to come.

He put the wet sheet to his face and breathed through it, to filter out the smoke and fumes. Then he felt panic rise in him and he stood and kicked at the door, but the lock wouldn't give.

From outside, through the window, came a red glow as the thatch caught and the night filled with flame. There was a crack like a gunshot as the glass of the small window shattered in the heat. The pane fell out and smashed into pieces on the floor. Instinctively he put his hands up to protect himself as fragments of glass sprayed around the room.

The smoke disappeared through the newly created gap, and fresh air surged in, but the air fed the flames and soon the thatch on the roof was burning brightly. He could hear the crackle of the straw.

Part of the ceiling fell with a crash on to the dresser and into the sink. It sizzled in the water. The tap went on running – water spilled out over the floor, but it made no difference to the inferno above.

She had to come soon. Had to come. Or maybe she wouldn't. Maybe she'd leave him there – evidence to be destroyed.

He suddenly realised that he was trapped in the room.

He had arranged his own cremation.

Perhaps he could burn the door first – burn his way through? But it was easier thought of than done. He pulled a piece of burning wood over, holding it by the part as yet untouched by flame. He held it at arm's length, trying to set light to the area around the lock, but it wouldn't take.

In desperation he lay on his back and began to kick and kick at the door with both his feet, looking like an infant having a tantrum.

She wasn't coming. She was going to leave him there.

The lower panel cracked. He kicked harder, again and again. It gave and splintered. He kicked at it more to make it wider. The gap created a through draught and fed the fire above him. It was rapidly spreading downwards – soon the whole roof would cave in.

He kicked the gap wider and tried to squirm through, but it was still too narrow. He pulled back, kicked again and again. Finally the central panel gave, he kicked it out and struggled through the gap, catching himself on splintered wood, gashing his arm badly.

But he was out. He knelt on the landing and caught his breath. Where was she? Where was Jonah? He could hear the fire raging above him, spreading through the thatch and into the timbers, moving as fast as a storm.

He got to his feet and edged down the staircase, one hand on the banister, one touching the wall, moving carefully down, half expecting to see her at any moment, the shotgun in her hands, staring up at him with hatred, saying, 'You just had to go and spoil everything for Matthew and me, didn't you?'

He kept moving. He reached the first floor and went on. He was down in the hallway now. There was nobody in the kitchen, but the door was open – as was another door, leading down to the cellar and basement. The door she had always kept locked.

He crossed to it. It was thick and reinforced with metal, and there was a second door behind it, to kill any sound that may have come up from the cellar. He heard her voice.

'Hurry, Matthew, hurry. There's a fire. You can't stay here.'

She had planned for everything, but not for this. Fire was the one thing that nobody could conceal. It broadcast its presence like a scream in the night. The burning roof would illuminate the sky for miles and miles. The farmers would see it, the motorists on the road, the lovers out for a late-night walk on the Tor. Someone would be ringing right now – several people – all making the same call. The men at the fire station would throw down their playing cards, grab their helmets and be buttoning up their uniforms as they ran to the vehicles.

The sirens would wail as the fire engines tore through the streets in the emptiness of the night.

Someone might see them and wonder where they were going – just as Jonah had seen and wondered, all that time ago. And Jonah, being Jonah, had run after the engine, with the mad notion that he could actually keep up with it, because he wanted to see the fire.

Here was the fire. Right here and now. Burning all around them.

'Hurry, Matthew, hurry, hurry…'

Joe backed away through the kitchen. The exterior door was open. He went out and into the yard. He looked up. The house was a torch now, a burning brazier. The animals were safe but afraid, the horses were whinnying, the sheep bleating and baaing for all they were worth.

He ran across to the stables, opened the door and slipped inside. He held the door to and peered out through the crack.

'Hurry, Matthew, hurry, hurry.'

She'd used the shackles again, fire or not. He hobbled alongside her as fast as he could go.

'The barn. We'll go to the barn. And not a word, you hear.'

Joe longed to call to him, to shout out his name, to yell, 'Jonah, over here, it's me!' But he dared not risk it and held his peace.

They disappeared into the barn. It was far enough away from the house to be safe – unless the wind blew up stronger and carried the fire over. But it seemed safe enough for now.

Come on, come on.

He willed them to come. Fire, police and ambulance. He willed them on, desperate to see the revolving blue lights and to hear the screaming sirens that would mean rescue and safety.

She came out of the barn – alone – then she ran back across the yard and re-entered the cottage. She came out moments later, carrying the shotgun.

'Where are you!'

Her voice echoed across the yard; her figure was illuminated by the flames.

'You had to spoil everything. There's always somebody to spoil it. Well, we'll see...'

He didn't move. The horses began to whinny again.

She heard them. She turned to face the stable, then walked towards it.

Then she stopped. She'd heard something else, and he heard it too. It was a siren, blazing a trail through the night.

She stood in the yard, indecisive, then she turned away from the stables and walked towards the gate. She opened it and swung it back. Then she sat down on the verge beside it, waiting for them to come.

The roof of the cottage was an inferno now, the flames swirling up into the sky, yellow and red and blue at the centre. The smell got into your nose and throat, the smoke choked your lungs.

A few minutes later two fire engines swung into the yard. The vehicles screeched to a halt and their crews jumped down. Some pulled out hoses, already connected to the tenders, and set about dousing the fire.

Others ran to the blazing building, shouting out – maybe people were trapped there. They called to the woman they had seen by the gate, but she didn't, or couldn't, answer them – shock maybe. Three men wearing fire suits and breathing apparatus tried to go inside the cottage, but by then the flames beat them back.

Two other firemen were searching in the yard for the water main. They found it and connected up another hose; a third cascade of water poured on to the pyre. Minutes after, an ambulance arrived, with a police car two seconds behind it. The ambulance men ran towards the burning building, calling to the firemen, 'Anybody in there? Anybody hurt?' The fire crews didn't think so, but they didn't know for sure.

Anna stayed where she was, mute and silent, sitting on the verge by the gate. Joe came out from the stables. He called to them all, to the police and the fire crews and the paramedics.

'The barn,' he yelled. 'Look in the barn!'

They looked at him in some kind of wonder, as if he had appeared from nowhere. Then two of the police, followed by two ambulance men, went into the barn. They expected to find animals maybe, in some kind of distress. They re-emerged, perplexed and bewildered, with a boy whose legs were shackled.

One of the police officers came to Joe. He stared at him, at his bloodied arms and torn clothes, at the mud and dirt on him, the smears of charcoal and soot, and at his wild eyes.

'What's going on here, son?'

He was a young man, little more than twenty-two or twenty-three. He removed his cap in order to wipe away the sweat from his forehead. His hair was fair, his eyes were sea blue – they reflected the flames of the fire.

'What's going on here, son?'

In as few words as possible, Joe told him. He pointed to the woman, sitting alone by the verge. She was rocking backwards and forwards, as if holding a small baby in her arms, and she was singing softly. A fireman stood a few feet away from her, watching her, ensuring that she was in no danger, but strangely hesitant to approach any nearer.

The young policeman walked over. He picked up the gun from where she had left it. She seemed to have no interest in it any more. He broke it open and removed the cartridge. He beckoned to a colleague to join him, and handed him the gun. Then he went to her.

'Ma'am...'

She looked up at him. She stared at him blankly, then suddenly smiled as if in recognition.

'Ma'am ... I think you'll have to come along with us now, please ...' She didn't move. 'I think you need to come along with us, if you would...'

The officer thought that she might go for him; he was afraid she would resist. But no. She stood up and smiled, extending her hand to him as if she wanted him to take it.

'Of course I'll come with you, Matthew,' she said. 'Wherever you want to go. My, but look how you've grown,' she said, 'so straight and strong, so tall and handsome, like I always knew you would.'

'Ma'am...?'

'Shall we go now, Matthew?'

'The car's just over here, ma'am, if you would.'

He let her take his hand and he led her towards the car. His colleagues watched with both suspicion and wonder.

'You've done so well, Matthew,' she said. 'I knew you would. You're a credit to your mother, the way you've turned out. I'm proud of you, I really am. You grew up so well, so kind and so good and so gentle.'

They came to the car. He opened the door for her. She hesitated a moment before she got in.

'I love you, Matthew,' she said. 'Very much.'

She seemed to be waiting for some kind of a response from him. He averted his eyes a moment and then looked back at her.

'We ought to be going now, ma'am,' he said.

'Mother,' she prompted.

He mumbled something under his breath. Whatever it was, she seemed satisfied.

'Don't forget your seat belt, please,' he said.

She smiled and nodded, and then she got into the car quite willingly, and put the seat belt on.

'Shall we go now?' she said. 'I'm ready. Will someone take care of the animals?'

The young policeman assured her that somebody would, and then the car drove away into the darkness. Behind them the firemen wound the hoses back on to the reels. Water dribbled from the nozzles on to the mud of the yard. The sheep went on bleating in their field. An owl dropped to the ground, scooped a small animal up in its claws and carried it off into the night.

It was three months later, at about eight twenty-five in the morning. Two boys, both in school uniform, both quite tall now and showing every sign of growing up, were walking to school. Each carried a backpack; the backpacks weren't identical, but they were pretty much the same.

They stopped and entered a newsagent's shop, which had a sign in the window saying, 'Only two school children at a time, please!' But they weren't there to do any shoplifting, they were just buying a few snacks before school. They weren't the shoplifting sort.

They soon re-emerged. One of them had a chocolate bar, the other a bag of salt-and-vinegar crisps.

As they ate and walked on, they heard a sudden commotion. From behind them came the loud wail of a siren. They stopped and turned to see a fire engine approaching. Cars were pulling to the side of the road to get out of its way. Pedestrians paused at the crossing to let it pass. It ran through a red light in its hurry to get to the emergency.

'Wonder where it's going?' one of the two boys said.

The other nodded and said, 'Yeah – I wonder. Whenever I see them, I always wonder where they're going.'

They were silent for an instant, and a look flashed between them. There was a moment then – a brief, fleeting moment – when, well, you just didn't know what might happen.

Then the moment flickered and died, like a spent match. One of the boys gave a wry, wistful smile and shrugged his backpack further up on to his shoulder to get it into a more comfortable position.

'Better get to school then,' he said.

'Yeah, sure. Better get to school,' his companion agreed.

They walked on down the road towards the railings and the red-brick building. The sound of the siren faded into the distance, like some Pied Piper of Hamelin trying to steal the children of the town away.

But they were wise to him and they didn't follow, though he called to them with all his heart as he ran away into the far hills, with his song trailing behind him.

Activities

Additional support for teaching these activities and assignments can be found on the Heinemann website at www.heinemann.co.uk

Preparation

1 As an introduction to his novel, the writer quotes from the 'Old Tale' of the Pied Piper of Hamelin. Read this quotation (page v).

   a **By yourself**, find information about the Pied Piper story from reference books or by using the internet.

   b **In pairs, i** compare the information you have found. Using your own words, tell each other the whole story. Keep stopping and handing over to your partner. You should each speak at least twice. Then, **ii** devise three freeze-frames which dramatise key points in the narrative. Act them to another pair. Then watch and comment on theirs.

   c Read Chapter 1 of *The Lost*. **In groups**, note down all the links you can find to the Pied Piper story, like this:

Chapter 1 of *The Lost*	The Pied Piper story
• 'It was as if the fire engine were a Pied Piper, and its siren and lights its song of enchantment' (page 4)	• The Piper enchants the children of Hamelin with his music: they have no choice but to follow it.

   d **As a class**, use your notes to predict what is going to happen in *The Lost* if it follows the outline of the Pied Piper story faithfully. In particular, talk about:

   • what might happen to Jonah ('He'd find it and, when he found it, there would be something important for him there' (pages 4–5))
   • which character in the Pied Piper story Joe could be like ('Joe stood where he was, out of breath, panting' (page 2))

2 The writer chooses 'Siren' as his title for Chapter 1. This refers to the siren of the fire engine. But it also refers to something else.

a **By yourself**, find information from reference books and/or the internet about the Sirens in Greek mythology.

b **In pairs**, write answers to these questions about the Sirens:

i what is *The Odyssey* (a book by the Greek writer Homer) about?

ii what did the Sirens look like?

iii where did they live?

iv why did all sailors fear them?

v why were Odysseus and the crew of his ship in grave danger?

vi how did Odysseus cunningly manage to avoid this danger?

c **By yourself**, make a large, coloured illustration of Odysseus sailing near to the Sirens. This could be drawn by hand or on the computer.

Then, in about 100 words, write or type your own version of how Odysseus was **i** lured by the Sirens and **ii** able to pass by them in safety.

Add what you write to your illustration: in it, around it, or under it.

d **In groups**, act out the story of Odysseus and the Sirens. **Either** improvise it, using dialogue and sound effects, **or** create freeze-frames showing key moments from the story.

e **As a class**, briefly discuss the links between the Sirens story and what happens in chapter 1 of *The Lost*.

Exploration

1 Build up character profiles of Jonah and Joe in Chapter 1:

a **In groups**, talk about which of these adjectives apply to each boy. Four of them fit Jonah best; four are more suited to Joe.

- adventurous
- loyal
- impulsive
- mature

- cautious
- imaginative
- anxious
- determined

Find evidence from Chapter 1 to back up your ideas.

b **By yourself**, make a character chart each for Jonah and Joe, to show your impressions of them. Use the **PEE** (**P**oint, **E**vidence, **E**xplanation) method. An example is given below:

Jonah		
Point	**Evidence**	**Explanation**
adventurous	'Jonah grinned and waved and then turned and ran on, haring off in the direction of the fire engine' (page 2)	Shows that Jonah likes excitement and follows his instincts: he does not think of possible dangers.

c Share your ideas with the **whole class**. Quote from your character charts to help you.

Then create a class 'master' chart for Jonah and Joe. Include any points about their characters you have noticed that are not on the list of adjectives in **a** above.

2 Read Chapter 2, 'The Stranger'.

'You weren't supposed to talk to strangers, everybody knew that' (page 7).

a **In pairs**, look carefully at the opening paragraphs of Chapter 2, down to '– why, even their names were alike'. Discuss: **i** why Joe is worried about Jonah and **ii** how Joe tries to persuade himself that Jonah is safe.

b **As a class**, examine one or two leaflets warning people of danger. They could be about road safety, unhealthy lifestyles, fire in the home, fireworks, burglary, etc.

Talk about how the leaflets try to inform and advise their readers. Focus on:

- general layout
- presentational devices – such as illustrations, the use of headings and sub-headings, bullet points, print size and the use of different fonts
- key words and emotive language
- paragraphs and sentence structures.

c **By yourself**, create a 'Stranger Danger' leaflet for children aged 7–9 to be given out in primary schools. Its language must suit the age group.

Your purposes are: **i** to *inform* them of the dangers and **ii** to *persuade* them not to talk to, or go with, strangers.

Your leaflet should use about 100 words and include illustrations. Use the techniques of language and presentation you studied in **b** above. If possible, produce it on a computer.

3 At the end of Chapter 2, the detective leading the search for Jonah makes a speech in a school assembly.

Plan, write and deliver her speech. Prepare for it like this:

a In pairs, note down all the *facts* that are known at this point about Jonah's disappearance. Collect them by skimming back through Chapters 1 and 2. (Remember, Joe has not told anyone about walking to school with Jonah, or about the fire engine.)

b By yourself, draft the first half of the detective's speech. As you do so, bear in mind these points from page 18, summarising **i** what she says and **ii** the way in which she says it:

- 'She repeated the appeal for help while simultaneously trying to be reassuring'
- 'She told everyone to be careful, but didn't want to panic anyone'
- 'There was no need to worry that anybody was going to get into any trouble'

c In pairs, practise delivering the first half of the speech. Your partner should listen carefully, and then make suggestions for change or improvement.

Redraft what you have written. Then draft the rest of the speech. Aim to make it last about three minutes altogether.

d In groups, listen to everyone's whole draft. Comment and make constructive criticisms, e.g.:

- Is it the right length?
- Are all the facts correct?
- Are the *language* and *tone* suitable for a large audience in a school assembly?
- Does it end on an appropriate note?

e In the light of your group discussion, **by yourself**, write out your final version of the speech. Then perform it on tape and/or to the class.

4 Use the following two passages from Chapters 3 and 4 for shared reading and writing:

- **Passage 1:** pages 32–3: from '"Don't worry, son…" the detective said' to '"They'll find him, Joe, they'll find him," his mother said'.
- **Passage 2:** pages 40–1: from 'The great sun was dipping down' to 'It was like it was your own, really – your very own son'.

a As a class, examine how in these passages the writer builds up: **i** a feeling of suspense and **ii** a sense of foreboding about what has happened to Jonah.

Focus on how the writer:

- makes us aware of time passing, fruitlessly
- takes us inside the mind of Joe (passage 1) and the searcher (passage 2) to show how anxiety about Jonah is increasing
- uses description of place and setting to create a mood of sadness and grief (passage 2)
- uses similes and metaphors to influence our feelings about the missing boy (in both passages).

b In groups, write a paragraph of your own to be added to passage 2. It will come immediately after '…for resale at the garden centres' (page 41).

This paragraph should:

- be about five sentences long
- describe other searchers looking for Jonah
- create a strong impression of the countryside: its vastness, its wildness, its physical features
- add to the forlorn atmosphere built up by the writer of the novel.

5   This activity is based on the two passages used for Activity 4.

   a   **In pairs,** choose **two** of these characters who appear in the passages:

   • Joe   • Joe's mother
   • the detective   • the searcher in passage 2

   Decide which of these characters each of you will be. Then take turns to be in the hot seat. Remember you have to think and feel like the character you have chosen in order to give convincing answers.

   Your partner will question you about:

   • what you think has happened to Jonah, and why
   • who you blame for his disappearance (it need not be just one person), and why
   • your personal feelings about his disappearance
   • what you expect the search for him will lead to.

   b   **As a class,** role-play a press conference held on the evening before Joe re-enacts his journey to school with Jonah. It is going to be transmitted on the 10 o'clock news. On the panel are:

   • the detective leading the search
   • Joe
   • the school's headmaster
   • Jonah's gran
   • one of the searchers from the local community.

   Choose five people to play these roles. The rest of your class are reporters from the local and national press, and from television. Plan your questions carefully.

   Note: the members of the panel will have different views and feelings. For instance:

   • what will be of most concern to Jonah's gran, as opposed to the headmaster?
   • how will the detective see things in a different light from Joe?

6 Read Chapter 5, 'The Alley'.

By yourself, choose to write **either** Joe's account in his diary of the re-enactment **or** the detective's report about it.

a If you choose to write Joe's diary, bear in mind:

- he will write in an informal style, using the first-person and his normal language
- he will include his feelings during the journey, not just the facts
- he will include his private thoughts about how much the re-enactment has helped in tracing Jonah.

His diary entry might begin something like this:

> The night before, I couldn't get to sleep. What if I bottled it? Or forgot the shop we went into to buy sweets? When did we first hear the siren? The police told me some TV people would be filming it all. I hated the idea of that, everybody watching. But they said that was the whole point – 'to jog people's memories'. I had to do it for Jonah.

b If you choose to write the detective's report, bear in mind:

- she will write in a formal style, using the third-person and impersonal language
- she will include only the facts of Joe's journey
- she will end her report by summing up how successful the re-enactment was from the police point of view.

Her report might begin something like this:

> The re-enactment of Jonah Byford's journey to school five days ago went largely according to plan. A police constable met Joseph Langley at his home at the agreed time, shortly after 8 a.m. After obtaining Mrs Langley's permission for the operation to proceed, he checked that Joseph had with him the same backpack Jonah was carrying on the morning he disappeared.

7 Read Chapters 8–12.

   a **In groups**, decide what impressions of Anna you get from these chapters. Do this by discussing in turn the following statements about Anna:

      1 She is the same as Joe's mother in character.

      2 She prefers her own company, and her animals, to other people.

      3 She likes Joe and goes out of her way to make him like her.

      4 She is very guarded about herself and may have some big secrets in her life.

      5 She believes strongly that dead people are 'lost' to us for ever.

      6 She does not really feel as friendly towards Joe as she wants him to think.

   Use the evidence of the text to say whether you think each statement is **true, false,** or **uncertain**.

   Show your findings by drawing speech bubbles and writing in the evidence, like this:

TRUE	FALSE	UNCERTAIN

1 She is the same as Joe's mother in character.

Evidence: _____

_____

_____

_____

_____

_____

| TRUE | FALSE | UNCERTAIN |

| 4 She is very guarded about herself and may have some big secrets in her life. | Evidence: _____
 _____
 _____
 _____
 _____
 _____ |

b **By yourself**, add any further impressions you get of Anna from Chapters 8–12. Draw your own speech bubbles and write in your evidence, as above.

c **As a class**, share your ideas. Then talk about what part you think Anna will play in the rest of the story.

d **By yourself**, imagine that Joe writes letters to his father (who moved to India when he and Joe's mother separated).

Write **two** of these letters:

- one in which Joe describes his first meeting with Anna
- one about any of his other visits to her farm in Chapters 9–12.

Bring out Joe's impressions of Anna. These may not be the same as the ones *you* have formed in working on **a**, **b** and **c** above.

8 'Towards the second anniversary of Jonah's disappearance, an enterprising journalist … wrote an article in one of the national newspapers asking where the boy was, what had happened to him and where the police investigation had gone wrong' (page 109).

By yourself, plan this article for publication in a tabloid newspaper. Prepare for it like this:

a Re-read the first eleven paragraphs of Chapter 11. They give you **i** information about what the article will say and **ii** an idea of its style and structure.

b Copy out the grid below. Then make notes on it for your article, using the three headings.

Facts	Who to interview	Who to criticise and for what

c **As a class**, read and annotate a photocopy of a tabloid newspaper article. Focus on:

- the headline: how does it grab your attention?
- the 1st paragraph: how many 'wh' questions does it answer?
- emotive language: what striking examples are there?
- powerful verbs and adjectives: what effects do they have?
- exaggeration and bias: how much can you find?
- quotations: why have they been chosen?

d **By yourself**, write your article under the headline 'Where Is He Now?' If possible, produce it on a computer.

9 Read Chapters 17–19.

Anna lives in an imaginary world. She has been doing so since her baby, Matthew, died at one day old. As Joe says on page 163, she is 'unbalanced by grief'.

a **In pairs**, put yourself in Anna's mind. Using what you find out in Chapters 17–19, answer the following questions as *if you are her*. Take turns to speak her answers.

  i What did you feel when 'they tried to take [your] baby away' straight after he was born?

  ii What happened when you found Matthew in the park, aged 3, and tried to bring him home?

  iii At the farmhouse, how did you prepare for the day when Matthew would come back to you?

  iv What did you do when Matthew arrived, saying he was lost after chasing a fire engine and feeling very thirsty?

  v For the last two years, how have you made sure Matthew knows you are his mother and that he develops like a normal teenage boy?

  vi How have you sometimes had to be strict with Matthew, for his own good?

  vii What did you think when the boy who called himself Joe started visiting you?

  viii Why did you have to keep Joe a prisoner, and what will you have to do with him now?

b **By yourself**, write *Anna's story* in the first person. See and present everything from her point of view. Start with the death of her baby, and end with her locking up Joe.

Most of your details will come from the story as you now understand it. You are free to add any others that fit in with what you know about Anna by the end of Chapter 19.

10 Read Chapter 20.

a **In pairs**, take turns to read aloud to each other pages 201–6, beginning from 'Here was the fire' and ending at '...and carried it off into the night'.

Imagine you are local newspaper reporters. You have to write up this part of the story for your front page, using about 250 words. Talk about: **i** which events you want to highlight, and which you want to leave out and **ii** who you want to interview, and why.

b **As a class**, look at a dramatic front page story from your own local newspaper. (These are often about natural disasters, daring rescues, miraculous escapes, or tragic deaths.)

Talk about:

- how the headline and first paragraph 'set up' the story
- how the reporter's choice of language makes it sound dramatic
- how quotations from people involved are worked in
- how the way the report is written plays on the reader's feelings
- how presentational devices, including photographs, add to the story's impact.

c **By yourself**, write for *The Torvale Chronicle* a front page story about how Joe, Jonah and Anna were found at the blazing farmhouse. Write between 200 and 250 words.

Use the techniques of writing you examined in **b** above. If possible, produce it on a computer. Make full use of presentational devices.

Inspiration

1 Look back over the novel as a whole.

  a **As a class**, exchange ideas about the main turning points or key moments in the novel's plot.

  To get you started, say why you would or would not include:
  - Jonah running after the fire-engine (Chapter 1)
  - Joe's re-enactment of Jonah's last journey (Chapter 5)
  - the discovery of Jonah's sweatshirt on a nearby beach (Chapter 6)
  - the seance Joe holds with David, Frea's nephew (Chapter 9)
  - the seance Joe holds with Anna (Chapter 14).

  b **In groups**, make an enlarged copy of the grid below.

The three major turning points in the plot of *The Lost*	
1 When…	because…
2 When…	because…
3 When…	because…

  After reaching agreement on your 'Top 3' turning points, fill in the grid. Make sure you put *detailed* explanations in each 'because' box. Use quotations from the story to back up your arguments.

  c **In class discussion**, each group should justify its choices. Afterwards, take a class vote to decide the 'Top 3' turning points. You should vote on **i** how well-reasoned the arguments put forward for them have been and **ii** how well these arguments have been backed up by reference to the text.

2   Look back over the novel as a whole.

By yourself:

a   Make notes about all the characters who are 'lost', or who feel a sense of loss, in the story. Use the spidergram below as a starting point. Then add further detail, evidence and explanation to it.

b   Use your notes to write an essay with the following title: Explain how several characters in the novel can be described as 'lost'. For which of them do you feel the greatest sympathy? Why?

Jonah

- disappears for two years
- in danger of losing his identity by being made to believe he is 'Matthew'
- loses two years of normal life by being without family, friends and school, etc.

Joe

- feels lost when his best friend vanishes without trace
- becomes 'lost' himself when, like Jonah, he is imprisoned by Anna
- in danger of losing his life when Anna plans to kill him and when he is forced to set the farmhouse on fire.

The Lost

Minor characters

- Jonah's father complains bitterly about his son's disappearance despite being estranged from him
- Joe's mother 'loses' Joe as he becomes drawn into Anna's world.

Anna

- suffers a tragic loss when her baby dies
- loses her grip on reality when she retreats into her imaginary world
- loses her sanity because of grief.

3 This activity asks you to work with a partner to write two short reviews of *The Lost*.

Websites exist on which young people can exchange opinions about the books they read.

With a partner, write **two** different reviews of *The Lost* for such a website.

- One should be from a reader of your own age who enjoyed the book.
- One should be from a reader of your own age who disliked it. Each should be about 150 words long.

Work in the way that suits you best. For instance, you could write one review each, or you could combine to write both reviews. What you *really* think about the book is less important than taking up a strong point of view **for** or **against** it.

Preparation:

a Read a selection of web-based book reviews by and for young people. How do they present a novel's storyline? How do they persuade readers to share the reviewer's opinion?

b Draft your two reviews. Show them to another pair and read theirs. Compare how your writing has turned out and make constructive comments.

c Redraft and produce final versions of your two reviews.

Decide which review best expresses your *true* opinion about *The Lost*. Post it on a suitable website for teenage readers.